"I'm not looking for forever. But I am looking for someday. I think I deserve that."

—Kate, from *Searching for Someday*

"You fought, survived, and flourished. You gave the world a big fuck-you and didn't let them break who you were. That's perfection, Kennedy. Sheer perfection."

—Nate, from *Searching for Perfect*

"Beautiful. I'm searching for something beautiful out there."

Her smile was pure joy and comfort and goodness. "Yes. And you've finally found it, my sweet boy. It's love."

—Wolfe and Mama Conte, from *Searching for Beautiful*

"Let me tell you exactly what I want, Arilyn, so we both know where we stand. I want you in my bed. I want to give you multiple orgasms, excruciating pleasure, and sleep with you at night. I'll take you to dinner and the movies and we'll date. And when we're no longer content or happy with the arrangement, we swear to be honest with the other and walk away with no lies. That's what I can offer."

"I agree."

He arched his brow. "That was quick. No thinking about it? We're very different."

"I know. But this isn't for always. It's only for the moment."

—Stone and Arilyn, from *Searching for Always*

"I don't want to hurt you, Ella."

"When you open yourself up to love someone, there's no way not to get hurt. You just have to decide if it's worth the pain."

—Connor and Ella, from *Searching for Mine*

ALSO BY JENNIFER PROBST

The Billionaire Builders Series

Everywhere and Every Way

Any Time, Any Place

All or Nothing at All

The Searching For Series

Searching for Someday

Searching for Perfect

"Searching for You" in *Baby, It's Cold Outside*

Searching for Beautiful

Searching for Always

The Marriage to a Billionaire Series

The Marriage Bargain

The Marriage Trap

The Marriage Mistake

The Marriage Merger

searching
for disaster

JENNIFER PROBST

POCKET BOOKS

New York   London   Toronto   Sydney   New Delhi

Pocket Books
An Imprint of Simon & Schuster, Inc.
1230 Avenue of the Americas
New York, NY 10020

First Pocket Books trade paperback edition July 2017

POCKET BOOKS and colophon are registered
trademarks of Simon & Schuster, Inc.

The Simon & Schuster Speakers Bureau can bring authors to
your live event. For more information or to book an event, contact
the Simon & Schuster Speakers Bureau at 1-866-248-3049
or visit our website at www.simonspeakers.com.

Manufactured in the United States of America

10 9 8 7 6 5 4 3 2 1

ISBN 978-1-5011-7826-9
ISBN 978-1-5011-4251-2 (ebook)

"All the suffering, stress, and addiction comes from not realizing you already are what you are looking for."
—Jon Kabat-Zinn

"And the day came when the risk to remain tight in a bud was more painful than the risk it took to blossom."
—Anaïs Nin

"Life is the sum of all your choices."
—Albert Camus

This one's for you, Dad.
I love you.

prologue

Six years ago

HE REMINDED HER of every delicious, forbidden, dirty action that could be committed under a tangle of sheets.

And tonight, he was going to be hers.

Isabella MacKenzie barely kept from licking her lips in anticipation of a feast. His golden movie-star looks should have put her off. She wasn't into pretty boys. She liked her men dark, dangerous, and tatted up. This one had no mar on his dusky-brown skin, and his white-blond hair gleamed like a halo gifted by the angels. He leaned against the wall, drinking a beer, a serene expression on his features. The party was loud and wild, with hookups galore played out amidst the screaming of alternative music, but he seemed untouched by his surroundings. He barely even glanced at the lineup of girls looking to offer themselves up for a night of forgetfulness. Her gaze flicked over his outfit. She preferred leather and old, tight Levi's. This one wore dark-washed designer jeans and a button-down ice-blue shirt with large cuffs pulled up to show a fancy design. His shoes were camel colored with ties and also looked expensive.

Definitely a mystery. One she wouldn't mind figuring out.

Because the demons had come for her again. Tickling her skin, whispering in her ear. That empty ache in her gut urged her forward, to do something to forget and take away the restlessness consistently taunting her. A night of forgetful, rowdy sex would help. And this time she wouldn't take the drugs. She didn't need them. Her best friend, Raven, was already suspicious, and she didn't want to lie. God knows she'd been lying enough to her own family. It wasn't fair to put that on the last relationship she had left.

Yes. This man would help her quiet the voices.

She headed across the room, making sure her generous hips swayed with enticement. It had become so easy now to become someone else. The seductress was like second nature, especially since she enjoyed her body and the pleasures it brought. She bucked the ridiculousness of the terms *slut* and *whore*, refusing to let civilization or stupid male viewpoints take something precious from her. Izzy enjoyed sex and picked who she wanted, when she wanted. It never lasted long anyway, but that was her choice. Her terms. She wasn't like her siblings, who craved a permanent relationship and ideals of love that didn't exist. She lived for the now and the excitement of dawn, where new possibilities always existed.

She stopped in front of him, cocking her head. His gaze had lit with a touch of interest. Up close, his eyes were pale, pale blue and so clear they reminded her of a still, serene lake touched with ice. His hair fell in thick, burnished, messy waves streaked with a dozen colors of light. His features were as classic as his clothes. Square chin. High cheekbones. Arched brows. Long, elegant nose. His lips were full and lush and looked so soft, she imagined her thumb skating over the plump flesh. Up close, he was even more beautiful, and her breath caught just a bit in admiration, as it would in front of Michelangelo's statue of David.

Or Chris Hemsworth as Thor.

"You don't belong here."

His gaze flicked over her, then swept back up again, lingering. "What gave it away?"

She shrugged. "You look bored. And you're too dressed up."

He regarded her with an honest curiosity she savored. "I think you're underdressed."

Izzy grinned at his pointed stare, which was taking in her beaded black crop top and low-cut jeans showing off her belly ring. She'd worked on her uncontrolled curls with a ruthless precision until the pin-straight strands framed her face with a bit of an edge. She sported purple streaks today because it matched her nail polish. "Usually that isn't considered a problem." His slight frown told her maybe it was. Interesting. "You don't go to college here, do you?"

The SUNY upstate campus was rural, with a solid education and a huge reputation for epic parties. Raven had dragged her here for the weekend for some type of art-and-wine festival in town, and they'd ended up hooking up with a cool group who invited them to crash at the dorms. Tammy and Rick were the party couple in the crew, quickly offering up Tammy's room to Izzy. Raven wanted to skip the college parties and head into town, so she'd left Izzy on her own for tonight.

"No. I graduated, but my brother lives in the dorms, so he invited me. You?"

"Nope. I just get invited to the parties."

They stared at each other for a moment. Izzy noticed immediately the instant connection simmering underneath the dialogue. Yes, there was chemistry. And he was different from the others. "How old are you?" she blurted out.

"Twenty-three." He glanced at the red Solo cup she held. "Tell me you're drinking age."

Her lips curved in amusement. "I am. Is that important to you?"

"That you're able to drink?"

She stepped forward, testing. "That we follow the rules."

His eyes darkened. The sounds around her dimmed to a foggy slur. "Nothing wrong with rules," he said softly.

"Nothing wrong with breaking them either."

The simmer caught and flared. Her heart ramped up as sweet sexual arousal sung in her blood, loosening her limbs and quieting her mind. How she loved the beginning of the chase; the excitement of the unknown gave her the perfect edge.

"What's your name?" he asked.

"Izzy."

"Short for Isabella?"

She nodded. "Yours?"

"William."

"Do they call you Willy?"

She gave him credit. Those gorgeous lips twitched in a half smile. "Not if they want to live. Friends call me Liam for short."

"Well, Liam. I'm crashing at a friend's place down the hall. It's quieter there. Want to go?"

Fascinated, she watched an array of emotions flicker across his face. "Is it safe to invite strange men to your room?"

With another man, she'd give in to the anger that he was judging her. But with him, she got the impression he really cared and didn't want her hurt. He seemed like the oldest twenty-three-year-old she'd ever met. "Are you safe?"

"Yes."

"Then let's go."

She didn't turn back to check if he was following. Threading through the crowds with expert ease, she exited and headed down the narrow hallway, where students spilled out, talking and laughing in a rowdy parody of

American Pie. She paused at the door with the plastic rose wrapped around the handle and went inside.

He followed her in.

The dorm room was small but clean and organized. Instead of the usual twin bed, this one was outfitted with a decent queen. Little else fit except for a nightstand and a battered chest of drawers. She switched on the bedside lamp and sat down on the bed.

He remained standing near the door. His sweeping gaze took in the surroundings, and Izzy sensed that this man noticed things others didn't. His mind seemed to actually click as if registering a level of detail most people ignored. Fascinated, she leaned back a bit and patted the bed. "Wanna come sit?"

"In a minute. Do you go to college somewhere else?"

"No. Not in college. I prefer a more worldly education."

He nodded, as if he agreed. "I don't think a freshman class could hold your interest," he noted. "You seem like you need more . . . color."

A chuckle escaped her lips. Yes, *color* was the perfect word. "I prefer travel to classrooms. People's experiences to books."

"A hands-on approach."

She deliberately stretched so her crop top strained against her breasts. She knew her body well, accepted its pros and cons with fairness rather than kindness. She'd always been a bit too short, a bit too curvy, but her breasts were definitely her best asset. Those pale-blue eyes regarded her with steadiness, but a lick of flame told her he wasn't immune. It had been a long time since she had enjoyed being a seductress on the hunt. "Definitely hands-on. In all ways."

"And smart."

"Wanna discuss my attributes a bit closer?"

"No."

Her brow lifted. "Changing your mind? I'm not looking to trap you in my lair if you don't want to be here."

"When I come over there, I'm going to do more than touch you, and there won't be any time for conversation. I'd like to get to know you a bit more first."

Her breath caught, then whooshed out in a rush. Damn, he was sexy. All serious and restrained, but a wildness lurked within him, ready to go off. She wanted to be the woman to uncork it. A current of tension hummed between them, but it was filled with the deliciousness of things to come.

"Most men despise talking," she said. "They prefer action."

"Action is important, but it's more powerful with the right information."

"What do you do, Liam?" Her curiosity was piqued. "Lawyer?"

His quick grin was charming and slightly lopsided. His front tooth held a tiny chip in the corner. She wondered how he'd gotten it. "Going into the police academy. That's why I'm here to visit my brother. Though I haven't seen much of him this weekend. At least he seems happy and settled here."

He was going to be a cop. The ultimate rule follower and disciplinarian king. A shudder of dislike hit her, but she still didn't want to tell him to go. He was too intriguing and she'd already made her decision to sleep with him.

She wanted him.

Now it was his turn to tilt his head and regard her. "Why do I feel I didn't impress you with my career choice?"

She shrugged. "Won't hold it against you. It's a lofty ambition. I wish you luck."

"Why don't you like cops?"

"Let's just say I believe societal restrictions are what's leaching the joy and creativity from life. Too many shoulds."

"But without certain rules, chaos erupts."

"Within chaos, truth can be found."

"'Art is the triumph over chaos,'" he quoted.

"John Cheever."

His gaze narrowed and probed. A funny tug at her tummy sent shivers of heat spreading through her. "Thought you didn't read."

"I like the internet and looking up weird things."

The hum grew to a crackle. Her body was already softening, anticipating the slide of his fingers over her bare skin, the hot thrust of his tongue between her lips. She waited for him to close the distance, but he hadn't finished the Q&A. His shift of weight hinted he was hard and a bit uncomfortable. Her gaze swept briefly downward to confirm the former.

Good.

"So, what do you do as a world traveler? Don't you need money, or do your parents finance you?"

The reminder of her parents zinged her heart. She tried so hard but always ended up hurting them. Whether it was poor grades, or the boys she picked to crush on, or the way she always got in trouble, their consistent disappointment shred her to pieces. It was much easier to leave so they could concentrate on her siblings. Her twin was the poster child of perfection. Between her brother being a doctor, her older sister running a successful bookstore, and her twin determined to be a surgeon, Izzy had nothing to bring to the table. She was the logo of ordinary. Worse, she didn't even want to try to be something more.

"Nope—I pay my own way. It's amazing how much you realize what you don't need in life. Most things that tie us down are useless stuff we want to collect, until it ends up collecting you and you find yourself trapped. I like traveling light."

"I never thought of it like that."

"I do. So, I stop and work for a bit at odd jobs, save up money, and hit the road to the next adventure."

"What type of odd jobs?"

"I learned bartending. Waitressing. Worked at the Gap.

Did hair at a local beauty parlor. Had a stint as a dancer."
At his blanch, she laughed. He was fun to try to shock. "Not
a stripper. Think *Flashdance*. I did some dance routines up
onstage in a bikini. But I really sucked, so that only lasted a
few weeks."

"You can't dance?"

"I tried to do a thing around the pole and crashed to the
floor, fracturing my ankle."

"Ouch."

"Yep. Very unsexy. Can't sing either. I'm tone-deaf."

The side of his mouth quirked. "Tragic."

"I did take off my clothes once for a job, though. An artist's model in France."

"So somewhere in the world your nude body is on a
canvas?"

"Maybe. Does that bother you? I'm getting the impression you're the stuffy type."

He didn't take offense. Amusement laced his features.
"My brother says the same thing. But I'm not judging, Isabella.
I'm actually fascinated. It's admirable to find your own way."

Her name fell like Mozart from his lips. His words held
no judgment, just truth. She relaxed. Already she'd shared
more of herself than ever before. Why did it feel so right?
As if they were protected in their own little bubble of comfort as they spoke. A cramped, plain dorm room ready to
hold both of their secrets.

"Did you always want to become a cop?" she asked.

"Yes," he said simply. "Always."

How lovely to know exactly what you wanted. Like her family. It seemed she hadn't received that lucky gene. "It must be nice to never question your path," she said softly. "To always know your direction."

"Sometimes. But I worry that, by being focused on one way, I missed all the interesting side roads that make life worth living."

His words hit her gut. She jerked slightly, and then the current was back, surging more intensely between them. Their gazes locked together, and for the first time, the raw intensity touched her so deep, her soul shuddered along with her body.

Then he moved.

It was like watching a graceful dance as he crossed the room to her. He owned his body and his intentions, reaching out to tug her up from the bed so she stood before him. Her head topped out midway up his chest. The subtle scents of cinnamon and mint clung to him, clean and sharp, and without thinking, she rose to her tiptoes and his head came down and he was kissing her.

His lips sipped, moving softly over her mouth as if feasting on an appetizer before the main course. His hands held her hips in a firm grip, his mouth moving over hers with a precision and control that was oh so sexy and real. She clung to his shoulders, digging her nails into the hard muscles, asking for more.

And he gave it.

Tongue plunging between the seam of her lips, he claimed her mouth without apology. Thrilling to his demands, she opened to him, swept away by the blistering heat of need between them.

Clothes fell off. He eased her onto the bed, cupping her bare breasts and tweaking her nipples, still not breaking the kiss. Every move was accented by the thrust of his tongue, coordinated with the smooth, exploring motions of fingers touching her everywhere, learning her texture and sensitive parts, until her thighs opened wider and wetness met his strokes, dampening his fingers.

One-night stands were usually drunken, intense, a bit clumsy. The race to an orgasm with a touch of savage fucking and the rippling, exciting cocktail of the unknown.

This was different. He touched her like they'd known each other before. Each hard muscle of his magnificent body fit to her curves. She arched and begged and gave more than she thought she had. The raging need for him grew and burned, twisting the knot inside of her tighter and tighter. When he finally broke the kiss, staring into her eyes with his wild, hungry blue ones, she clutched his shoulders in sudden panic.

"Too much," she whispered frantically. "Too—"

"I know." His voice was a growl of sound. Sweat beaded on his forehead. Golden hair fell across his brow in burnished glory. Those lush lips curled in fierce demand. "Don't stop me. Don't stop this."

"Liam."

He bent his head, sliding down her body. Eased her legs wider apart. And covered her throbbing center with his warm, wet mouth.

He took her higher and higher. She curled her toes into the mattress, helpless to fight the waves of the climax building inside, until the tension was drawn so fine, her body stiffened with agony. His tongue swept over her hardened clit again. Soft lips suckled. Fingers curled and worked her, and then she hovered on the precipice, craving to go over and too afraid to take the plunge.

"Come for me, Isabella."

His command propelled her forward, the climax seizing every muscle as she bucked and cried out, his hands holding her tightly to the mattress in a delicious bond of restraint.

The sound of a ripping wrapper hit the air. He reared up, looking into her face, pausing at her dripping entrance.

"Again."

He surged forward, inch by inch, filling her completely. The stretching of interior muscles, the burning heat of him, the bruises on her hips as he held her tight for his invasion— all of it blew through her mind and scattered to the wind under the sheer intensity of his claiming.

Izzy studied his gorgeous face. Jaw tight with tension, biceps flexed, skin damp with sweat, he fucked her with a merciless beauty she knew she'd never forget. He owned her in that moment like no man before, and Izzy had a stream of startling thoughts right before the second climax exploded through her.

Rightness.

Belonging.

Silence.

Then she closed her eyes and let go.

IZZY HAD SEX in order to stop the chaos.

But sex with Liam was different.

She was used to parting quickly afterward. Rarely did she stay the night to sleep or spend too long cuddling. She lacked a part of intimacy most women seemed to be built with and preferred to go off on her own after her satisfaction, usually falling into a deep, pleasant slumber.

This time she found herself wrapped around him. Head on chest. Leg squeezed between his thighs. Arm draped over his shoulder. How long had passed in comfortable silence? Fifteen minutes? Half an hour? She didn't know. Instead of inane conversation or comments about how good it had been or a speedy exit, they just lay together, not speaking.

"Whose room is this?"

His voice was a whisper in her ear. She smiled in the dark. "A girl named Tammy. I just met her, but she let me use her room."

"So there are no crazy boyfriends stalking you, ready to beat my ass?"

Izzy didn't do boyfriends.

Until now.

Not that she was getting caught up in the great sex or anything. It was more of a feeling inside than a physical urge. Something had shifted. Liam seemed able to quiet all those messy tendrils of unsettlement.

"No. I move around too much to drag a man with me."

"What's next on your itinerary?"

She loved the way he spoke—elegant and cultured, as if he weren't naked in bed with her and hadn't done dirty, delicious things to make her scream. "Not sure. Probably get a job for a while. Save some money."

"Manhattan has tons of opportunity for work."

She stiffened but kept her voice casual. "Manhattan, huh?"

"Yep. I'm heading there next week for the academy. Lined up a decent place. There's plenty of culture, and restaurants, and . . . dancing opportunities."

She couldn't help it. She laughed, then twisted around to meet his gaze. "We just met, screwed, and now you're asking me to follow you to the city while you train to be a cop?"

He winced. "I don't like the word *screw*."

"Where did you come from, Liam?"

He sighed. "That's what my brother asks me a lot."

"Inviting a strange woman into your life can be dangerous."

His full lips parted in a smile as she used his own words against him. "Maybe I'm a dangerous type of guy. Maybe I'm ready for my own adventure." His finger traced the curve of her cheek, the line of her jaw. His blue eyes filled with a tenderness she hadn't seen in a very long time. This man had a heart and soul to give some lucky woman. He didn't realize how broken she was. How trouble stuck to her very aura like static cling.

But oh, how her heart suddenly leaped in her chest. To be with him for as long as it lasted. Or at least a little while longer. "I'm not good at commitments."

"Not asking for one."

"What are you asking for, then?"

"Time."

Yes. Time. What a perfect answer to satisfy both of them. Time to explore, grow closer, grow apart. She'd talk to Raven. Her friend had been getting itchy herself lately— looking to settle down into a more permanent job. Maybe this would be a good opportunity. "I've been wanting to spend some time working on my comedy routines. They have tons of clubs there ripe for a new stint."

He blinked. "Are you funny?"

She sighed. "Not really. But it's been on my bucket list."

His smile reminded her of sunshine and rainbows after a hard rain. "Then I'll sit in the audience of the improv and arrest anyone who tries to throw rotten apples at you."

She giggled. Izzy hadn't known she had any giggles left

from her childhood. Somehow he'd wrested one out of her. His eyes blazed blue flames and he lowered his head to kiss her again.

A loud banging filled the air. "Izzy! Open up; it's Rick. Got something for you."

"Hang on a sec." She looked around for something to cover herself with, finally grabbing a ratty blue blanket and wrapping it tightly around her body. She opened the door a few inches and peeked out.

Rick grinned. His ginger hair, pale skin, and black-framed glasses made him look more like a professor than a student. "Hey, Izzy. Bunch of people been looking for you."

"Sorry, I'm tied up. Does Tammy need me? Or Raven?"

His gaze probed the empty space, then he gave a knowing laugh. "Ah, got it. When you're done being tied up, come to room 3A. Tammy wants to hang with you. For now, here's a start-up. Consider it a freebie."

He shoved the brown paper bag at her.

She grabbed it.

Then trembled. Her fingers clutched it with sheer possessiveness but she tried to fight the impulse. "Umm, I don't need this right now. Thanks anyway."

The knowledge in his eyes held no mockery or judgment. "Sure you don't. Like I said, it's just a gift. For now."

"But—"

He turned and walked away, leaving the bag behind.

Izzy shut the door and dropped the package on the table. Stared at it for a moment. She didn't have to open it. It wasn't a big deal that she happened to like some weed now and then like most of the population. Sure, she'd done some coke, too, but she had things under control. Wasn't like she was a meth head, and hell knows she didn't shoot anything up. Needles were a deal breaker.

Freebie.

Her fingers shook slightly as she removed the contents and registered what she held. The small vial of pure-white powder beckoned. Not now, of course. She'd wait till the bad stuff crept in her head again, and a simple sniff would push it all away for a long time. Was it so terrible to need a bit of help to cope?

And afterward, she not only coped. She excelled. She was smarter and clearer and happy. People used drugs all the time, whether it be antidepressants, or weed, or over-the-counter cold meds. Some drank. She took a bit of cocaine now and then. No big deal.

"Isabella? Are you okay?"

She shoved the vial back and turned with a smile. "Sorry, just some friends checking on me."

"What's in the bag?"

She tossed it toward the back of the table and dropped the blanket. "Not important. I'm sorry we got interrupted." Knowing she had a wonderful secret that was waiting for her, she was hungry for more of him. Hungry for his mouth and skin, to tumble back to the mattress and embrace the way he filled her up. She dropped one knee on the bed.

Instead of pulling her close, he sat up with a frown. His mussed hair gave bed head a sexy new image. "You look different. What's in the bag?"

She paused. Studied him. What was he doing? Why was he obsessing over her personal business? Her voice became edged with razor sharpness. "It's nothing, Liam. Forget it. Why are you making such a big deal out of a bag?"

"If it's not a big deal, why don't you tell me what's in it?"

The world narrowed. Resentment slithered like snakes within her. She hated people ordering her around and telling her what was good and what wasn't. She'd earned a right to do what she wanted without answering questions. Izzy backed away from the bed and rewrapped the blanket around her. Warning bells clanged loudly in her head. "Because it's not your business. We may have had sex, but you haven't earned the right to pry. What's really going on?"

His stare shredded her barriers and buried deep. Her heart beat as loudly as the warning bells. How did this man seem to know her so well when they had just met? As if he sensed she was nearing a precipice and he'd decided to yank her back.

"Are there drugs in the bag?"

She raised her chin, blood chilling in her veins. "Back off, Liam."

"I don't do drugs, and I don't surround myself with people who do. I've seen firsthand how that stuff ruins lives and turns people into monsters."

Izzy forced a laugh but her throat was bone-dry, and it came out a bit rattled. "'Monsters'? Don't you think you're taking this law enforcement thing a bit too far? You're telling me you never did a bit of weed in high school or college? Drank underage? Stolen a cig before you were eighteen? Must be nice to be perfect."

His jaw tightened. "I wouldn't know; I'm not perfect. I'm also not about to gamble with my life either. Listen, just get rid of the bag. You don't need it."

"You don't have the right to tell me what to do."

His gaze burned. "Maybe not, but I'm asking. Something happened between us tonight. I'm not into magic and bullshit, but there's a connection I feel with you I want to explore. I can't do that if the stuff in that bag is more important than me. Toss it, Izzy. I'm asking."

The tiny room tilted around her as shock hit. She had just met him, and he was asking her for a sacrifice. Wasn't it really just a way to control her? Shouldn't he be willing and able to accept her exactly the way she was? After all, she wasn't a druggie. She liked to take an occasional hit of coke. Why was that so wrong?

As she stared at him, the room filled with a rising tension and inner battle of wills. The bag behind her became a symbol of what path to choose. Yes, she'd never experienced such a physical encounter, one that seemed to raise sex to a higher level into the mental and emotional. But she refused to allow him to set rules. She could get rid of the bag if she wanted to. That wasn't a problem. The bag had no power over her.

But she didn't want to.

Izzy stepped back, as if to protect the item she'd sacrificed the unknown for. "No, Liam. I'm asking you to let it go. Just trust me—it isn't a big deal."

Slowly, the knowledge that she'd already chosen leaked into his eyes. He jerked away, a flash of pain carved in his face before it was quickly smoothed over by a distant expression. He nodded. Rose from the bed. And dressed.

"I'm not going down this road, Isabella," he said softly. "I'm not built for it, and I'm not about to watch what happens next." He paused, hand on the knob. "See ya."

He left.

Izzy stood still in the empty, silent room. Slowly, the bitter rage swept in from deep inside and caught her in its vicious grip. It might be the enemy but it was what she'd known and lived with her entire life. In a way, it was safe, so she embraced the violent emotions with zeal.

How dare he give her ultimatums. He was like all the others. Judgmental. Arrogant. Only able to make decisions based on logic rather than accept the unknown chaos life demanded, and she was better than that.

Better than him.

Filled with righteous rage, she tore open the bag and grabbed the vial. The blindingly white powder beckoned and promised forgetfulness. Justice.

Silence.

Izzy unscrewed the vial.

one

"KINNECTIONS MATCHMAKING AGENCY. May I help you?"

Gulping, feminine sounds burst from the other end of the phone. Grabbing her pen, Izzy scribbled down notes, making soothing noises and quickly bringing up the woman's profile on the computer.

"Yes, Hailey, I have your screen profile right here. You had a date with Gary last night and—oh, he didn't pick up the check? No, I agree there's no excuse. Did you offer to pay? Well, if you offered and he agreed, it wasn't a deliberate ploy to force you to take care of him. Gary is a people pleaser, so he may have thought you were intent on showing him you're completely independent."

As the client rambled on about gigolos and being taken advantage of, Izzy smiled at the tall blonde who walked in, looking nervous and excited. The second and third phone lines lit up and the fax machine shuddered, spitting out page after page of profiles.

"I don't think you should be hasty, Hailey," she said in

her best soothing tone. "We matched you with Gary after an extensive profiling, and he already called to let us know he can't wait to call you for another date. Said you were beautiful and charming." The startled pause on the line told her she'd hit the real problem. Hailey's confidence had been shattered by a previous breakup. Arilyn had been working with her in therapy, but first dates were extremely difficult for her.

The tone of the conversation immediately changed. Hailey burst into a detailed description of the date and how she really liked Gary and would give him another chance to pay. Izzy made a note on the chart, wrapped up the phone call, took care of the other messages, and motioned the new client over.

"Welcome to Kinnections. Are you here to see Kate?"

The woman nodded. "Yes. I have a session scheduled."

"We're so happy you're here. Can I get you some coffee or tea? Water?"

"No, thank you. I'm too nervous."

Izzy smiled with encouragement. "Nerves are good. It reminds us we're alive and taking a step toward changing our life." She glanced at the schedule. "Shelby, right?"

"Yes. I like that philosophy. Makes me feel more empowered."

"Our mental state is the most important obstacle in dating and relationships." Izzy buzzed Kate, then handed the client a clipboard with a lengthy questionnaire. "You're in good hands with Kinnections."

"My friend was matched here and she's so happy. I just feel, well, I'm ready, you know? Ready to find someone to share things with."

"I know exactly what you mean." Izzy kept the smile on her face, but inside she ached. How long had it been since a man held her? Touched her? Hell, even taken her to dinner or the movies?

Too long.

Yet maybe not long enough.

The click of heels made her turn. Kate stood next to her desk dressed in her usual black pantsuit, her silver hair swinging under her chin in a smart, sleek bob. She was the epitome of a polished businesswoman, yet warmth infused her voice. Kate was one of the three owners of Kinnections, and Izzy was consistently impressed with Kate's ability to balance the high emotions intrinsic to a matchmaking business with the practical ability to make rational decisions.

"Good to see you again, Shelby. I'm looking forward to the beginning of your journey with Kinnections. We'll be going into the first room on the left. Why don't you take a seat, start on the questionnaire, and I'll be right there?"

Shelby nodded and disappeared.

"How are you doing, Izzy? I feel like we didn't even get to say good morning to each other."

Izzy grinned. "Because the moment nine a.m. comes, we're slammed. Ever since Kinnections was dubbed the "love fix" in *Cosmopolitan* magazine, there's no such thing as downtime. I don't know how you three are managing."

"Ugh, I really hate that term they stuck on us, but Kennedy said it was marketing genius that doubled our client base." As a co-owner of Kinnections, Kennedy was in charge of the makeovers, social media, and marketing. Arilyn was the third woman in the powerful trio, and she concentrated on computer matching and therapy for all of the clients. Together, they had created a dynamic, profitable business and were still close like sisters.

"You don't like being called a love doctor?" Izzy teased.

Kate winced. "It's awful. Even worse with it spread all over Facebook and Instagram in our ads."

"Ah, but that's because I'm a genius." Kennedy's throaty voice cut through the air. "We made a crapload of money and we're so busy Arilyn couldn't take on teaching another anger management course. You should be thanking me."

Izzy took in her apple-green Michael Kors suit, Jimmy Choo pumps, and Kate Spade bag. With her thick caramel-colored hair and flawless appearance, she was a driving force both in the company and with anyone she came into contact with. Izzy adored her smart-ass demeanor and wicked sense of humor. Kate lifted her brow. "I hate it and refuse to thank you. You made us post our pictures on the banner!"

Kennedy flashed a smug grin. "Of course. We're all super hot, so that sells both females and males. I would've put the dogs on there, too, but Arilyn gave me some crap about animal rights."

A third voice joined the mix, the tone low and melodic. "I refuse to allow Pinky or Robert to be exploited in your quest for money," Arilyn said firmly. Her long, straight red hair fell to her waist, and she was dressed in her usual organic-cotton yoga pants and shirt. "We can hardly keep up with our client base to begin with."

The final member of the trio, Arilyn was a huge animal rescue advocate, vegetarian, counselor, and one of the most giving, beautiful women Izzy had ever met. She brought a calm balance to the team.

"Thank goodness we hired you, Izzy," Kate said. "The last receptionist was trying to poach dates from the system. Too bad your sister went back to surgery. She could've been a master matchmaker."

Her twin, Genevieve, had briefly worked at Kinnections when she decided to leave her career in medicine, but then she realized being a surgeon was her true calling. Izzy was grateful the team had taken a chance with her, on Gen's recommendation. She'd hurt a lot of people in the past few years, including her twin, but Gen had welcomed her back into her life with open arms. Emotion choked her throat. Her entire family had been forgiving and ready to take a chance on her again. She'd sworn to never let them down.

"I appreciate you hiring me," she said quietly. "I know I hadn't done much to earn your trust, but I really love working here."

Arilyn patted her shoulder. "We all deserve second chances. I know it's only been a month, but I've been so impressed. Not only with the way you handle the clients, but your computer skills are off the hook."

She shrugged. "I've always been good with computers. I like fooling around."

"Well, I was wondering if you'd like to take on another project. I just can't seem to handle the workload any longer, and I need someone to double-check the new spreadsheets and data I fed into the system."

Pleasure speared her. It had been a long time since she excelled at anything besides waitressing or selling makeup. "I'd love to help."

Kennedy tilted her head and studied her. "When are you going to let us hook you up, babe? Don't you think it's time?"

Izzy wondered if she'd ever again feel ready to have a relationship. Then again, that had been the reason she avoided entanglements in the first place. Much easier to make drugs her one and only lover. They were a possessive, jealous, and demanding partner. She'd passed her two-year anniversary drug-free and built a solid, comforting life for herself. Even her mentor agreed she could begin to test the dating waters, but for the first time ever, Izzy enjoyed the boredom. She'd become everything she once detested, trapped in a regular routine with no additional color.

She was finally at a certain level of peace.

Izzy waved a hand in the air and laughed. "Thanks for the thought, but I'm good. I am thinking of getting a dog, though."

Arilyn clapped her hands together. "I'm so excited! Just tell me when and I'll take you to Animals Alive. They have so many sweet dogs there needing a home."

Kennedy rolled her eyes. "Was thinking more of a six-foot-five hunk of a blond keeping her warm at night. Hey, what about Stone's partner, Devine? He's single. And H-O-T."

Izzy spoke up. "Umm, guys—"

"I never thought of Devine!" Kate jumped in. "I can't believe they still haven't met. He may be perfect to test the waters, Izzy. He's good-looking and really nice. Not too nice."

"The perfect mix of nice," Kennedy said.

Izzy tried again. "I'm not—"

"I cannot believe I'm saying this, but Devine may be a great match for her," Arilyn said slowly. "Stone said he's not seeing anyone right now but has been looking to settle in with someone."

Izzy gulped. "What?"

"Oh, not marriage or jumping into anything," Arilyn corrected. "But I think he's getting tired of endlessly dating and not making a connection. It may be worth a try. I can have Stone bring him by after his shift. Test the chemistry between you."

"Definitely," Kennedy said.

"Agreed," Kate said.

"No."

They looked at her in sheer surprise. Izzy shook her head. "I'm sorry, and I'm truly grateful for the love doctors trying to hook me up, but I'm still not ready. I don't want the pressure."

Uh-oh. Three women's gazes echoed a determination she wasn't used to dealing with. They shared a glance, then nodded in unison.

"We understand," Arilyn said.

Kennedy held her hands up in surrender. "No problem. We just figured we'd try."

Kate didn't say anything.

Suspicion formed, but it wasn't the time to push. "Kate, I think you forgot that Shelby's waiting for you."

Kate clapped her hand over her mouth. "Oh my goodness! Thanks, Izzy—check in with you later."

She raced away, shutting the door behind her, and Izzy faced the two remaining partners. Originally Genevieve's close friends, Izzy now felt as if a bond had formed and she was finally able to consider them as more than just her employers. They'd accepted her fully without hesitation and let her prove herself with her work.

Kennedy sighed. "I'm telling you, babe. Devine is divine. You'll thank me."

"No, thank you."

Arilyn laughed at Ken's disappointment. "Give her time. I believe in fate and the power of energy guiding us in the right direction. Maybe there's another way for her to meet someone other than Kinnections, or setting her up with Devine."

"What's better than Kinnections?"

"What about Earth Mother?"

Arilyn's odd response made Kennedy stiffen. Shock gleamed in her whiskey eyes, and suddenly a giant, smug grin curved her lips. "Gotcha. You're so smart, A."

Arilyn sighed. "I know. But right now I have to prep for my next session, then get back home to feed Pinky. See you guys later."

Izzy said good-bye, turning toward Kennedy for answers. "Okay, what's going on? Who's Earth Mother?"

Kennedy practically oozed fake innocence. "Oh, never mind. It's nothing. I have to go, too. See ya."

She shot out of Kinnections, leaving Izzy more confused and a tad bit curious. She should've known these three would be obsessed with hooking her up. Not only did they run a matchmaking agency, but they were all happily involved with gorgeous men who were also kind. Did they even make such combinations in the male species anymore?

The phone rang, the doorbell chirped, and Izzy pushed the thought out of her mind, focusing on work.

two

"Y OU'VE BEEN AWAY on vacation and you still haven't gotten laid?"

Officer William Devine regarded his partner with annoyance. "Why are you stuck on my love life all of a sudden? It was a family vacation. My brother was getting married."

Officer Stone Petty snorted. He sat in the passenger seat of the squad car, his gaze assessing their surroundings, looking for any type of action that would perk up their day in Verily. His head almost hit the ceiling of the car. With his staggering height, coal-black hair, craggy features, and goatee, Stone easily intimidated perps. They made the perfect team of bad cop/good cop and it had been working for a few years now. Besides being a great cop, Stone was an actual friend he trusted with his life. "There must've been a pretty bridesmaid or flower girl or someone."

"Flower girls are usually young girls."

"Maid of honor, then. Or matron—whatever. Chicks love to get laid at weddings."

Amusement made his lips twitch. Even after years of being partners, Stone still was able to make him laugh. "When was the last time you got laid at a wedding?"

His friend puffed up like a proud cock. "Recently. At Kate's wedding. That's when Arilyn and I really hooked up."

"Doesn't count. You were already in a relationship with her."

"Semantics. And I'm not stuck on your love life. I've just noticed you've been a bit bitchy lately, and with men, that channels itself into one direction. The almighty dick."

Devine shook his head. "Not bitchy. Just restless. I don't know; it's stupid."

"Try me. Looks like everyone's obeying the law, so we have time to kill."

True. Verily was a small upstate town located on the Hudson River in New York. It held a quaint main street complete with cafés, wine bars, bakeries, a dog park, and a bunch of artist shops. On a warm September evening, as dusk fell over the valley, touched by a blend of color from the leaves just beginning to turn, the view of the majestic mountains was breathtaking. Jagged, shadowed cliffs rose up from the river, with Verily squeezed right in the middle, like a jewel encased in gold.

Unfortunately, there wasn't much crime in the town. A drunken brawl, speeding ticket, or weed bust kept them occupied, but they were never going to see the hard-core action one of the city boroughs would. Stone had come from the Bronx originally before transferring to Verily, and had some tough issues to deal with.

Devine used to love the fact he could do his part without burning out or losing his faith in humanity. Too many of his fellow officers did, especially after 9/11. But lately an itch crawled under his skin, urging him to break out of his usual routine and do something different.

Something crazy.

But he didn't do crazy. Never had, never will.

He tried to explain in words that didn't even make sense to him. "Maybe I'm going through some weird midlife crisis. I watched my brother get married and he's so damn happy. Hell, even *you're* happy, and I never would've bet the ranch on Arilyn loving your sorry ass."

Stone grunted. "So, you want to find your love match or something? Why don't you let Arilyn hook you up with Kinnections?"

"Hell, no. That's humiliating. I don't need an agency to find a date."

"Not talking about a date—you've found plenty of those. Talking about a real match with a woman you can connect with. Maybe that's why you're restless."

Devine stared at his partner in shock. Damned if his once surly, sarcastic, sometimes mean-tempered friend had gotten bit by the love bug. Now he was shitting sunshine. "You're scaring me."

Stone shrugged. "I'm happy. Sue me for wanting you to be happy, too."

Devine couldn't argue with that statement. His friend deserved everything he had finally found with Arilyn—and their rescue Chihuahua, Pinky. He'd missed both of them during his family trip. He'd missed his job, too, and Ray's Billiards where he hung out, and the life he had built here.

Then why did he feel so lost?

He rubbed his temple and forced the thought aside. Maybe Stone was right. Maybe he needed to connect with a woman on a deeper level and not just scratch a physical itch. He'd dated plenty of nice women and usually had his pick. Quantity wasn't the problem and never had been.

It was quality. Especially with the type he kept searching for but couldn't seem to find.

The shimmer of memory caught him like a sucker punch. Not her again. It was ridiculous how a silly one-night stand still affected him years later. Probably the lure of the unknown. It was easy to spin tales of what could have been and not deal with the reality. They'd barely known each other, and after a week together they would have probably broken up.

Yet her scent and face still haunted him. He'd just learned to live with it.

"Just think about joining Kinnections. You may find what you've been looking for. Sometimes you gotta do something different. Mix things up."

Devine agreed. He was stuck in a cycle that was pleasant and comfortable but lacking. "Do I have to go through counseling?"

Stone groaned. "That would suck. Arilyn probably wouldn't do it, because she knows you too well. Maybe I can get her to sneak you a free pass and you can just start hooking up right away."

"Yeah. Okay, why don't you talk to her for me and see first?"

"No problem. I'll use my charm and sex appeal and you'll slide right through the door with none of that bullshit they put the other guys through. Hey, look at the white Ford Taurus. Taillights out!"

Devine hit the lights and sped up. "Think maybe there's a body in the trunk? Or drugs in the glove compartment?"

"Let's find out."

As Devine chased the Taurus, he wondered if Kinnections could help him finally get out of his rut.

IZZY CURLED UP on the worn ice-blue sofa, cradling a mug of green tea in her hands. The television hummed low in the background, but the cottage held a quiet hush filled with peace and comfort.

She'd been lucky. Arilyn had gotten engaged and moved in with Stone, which left her twin's bungalow in Verily open. Izzy had moved in and for the first time in years felt like she'd found home.

Everything in the cottage held an old-fashioned flair, from the white shutters, crooked porch, and cheery furniture in canary yellow and ice blue. The kitchen nook held a counter and stools, and a square table for bigger meals. The plank wood floors held colorful braided throw rugs. She'd fallen in love with Verily and its artistic patrons, slowly building relationships with the local bakers and shop owners.

When had she ever been happy to stay home in the evening? When had the haunting voices finally stopped pushing her toward the next unknown road in a quest for an adventure, good or bad? Izzy tried not to question herself too much. She liked the person she was still becoming, finally clean and sober for two years now. It had taken her a long time to rebuild her family's and friends' trust, but with time, amends, and a willingness to face her demons, she was in a good place. Now, with her job at Kinnections challenging her mind, the final piece had slid into place. She'd spent so many years doing dead-end jobs with no thought of the future. Maybe if she proved herself with her computer skills, she'd be able to really hone her talent and help her friends.

She sipped at her tea and decided to watch *Star Wars: A New Hope* again. Her obsession with the *Star Wars* franchise bordered a tiny bit on the obsessive, but who cared? Her sister Alexa was crazed over the New York Mets. There was something so beautiful and almost poetic about the battle between good and evil, and she refused to apologize to anyone.

She slipped in the DVD, settled back, and relaxed.

Until the knock came from the door.

Frowning, she put down her mug and peeked through the windows. A smile curved her lips and she flung the door open. "What are you doing here?"

Her twin sister, Genevieve, walked in holding a paper bag. She was still dressed in her scrubs, and her face reflected a happy weariness from her job as a surgeon. Of course, the thing in life that really made her smile was Wolfe. Her best friend turned lover held the key to both her heart and soul. Izzy had never seen a couple so perfectly matched, as if two halves had actually formed a whole.

"I got out of the hospital early and wanted to stop in to see you. And I brought biscotti!"

"Oh God, the caramel pecan?"

"Yes. And the chocolate."

"Want some tea?"

Gen wrinkled her nose. She was a hard-core coffee drinker. "No thanks. Just the sugar, please."

Izzy grabbed two plates and her sister laid the pastries out. They both sighed and stared at them for a while. Even when they were young, they loved sugar and dessert and got into fights with their mother regarding second and third helpings. Then again, it was mostly Izzy who got in trouble. Gen always backed down, not wanting to get their mom mad, but Izzy didn't care and always forged ahead with no caution.

"Are you seriously watching that movie again? You've memorized every line!"

Izzy stuck out her tongue at her sister. "It has hot men and cool women with lightsabers. How can you not love it?"

Gen laughed. "Fine, I give up. I can see you naming your kids Luke and Leia when you have them."

"I actually love that idea."

Gen groaned. "Forget I mentioned it. How've you been doing?" Her sister took a bite of her biscotti and closed her eyes in pleasure. "Kate said you're killing it at work. Everyone's impressed at your learning curve. Did you ever work at a matchmaking agency before?"

Izzy bit into the cookie and moaned. Perfect firm texture. A touch of sweetness. The crunch of pecan. Best thing ever. "No, but I have people skills. Well, I found I had better people skills when I wasn't high, but I think all the traveling helped me deal with a wide variety of people."

"Yeah, I can see that. You always were the one who could convince people to do stuff. And you have a worldly flair about you that's new."

Izzy raised her brow. "Worldly flair? Oh boy, what do you want, Gen?"

Her sister burst into laughter. "Well, now that you mention it . . ."

"You're not going to jump on the Devine bandwagon, too, are you?"

Gen frowned. "What do you mean? What does Stone's partner have to do with anything?"

Izzy waved a hand in the air. Then took another bite. "Nothing. Kennedy was trying to set me up with Devine, saying I need to begin dating. I told her no, but I thought maybe you were here to convince me."

"Hmm, I never really thought about Devine. He's hot, but I was always too fascinated with Stone and Arilyn's fireworks to really concentrate on him. Maybe he's worth a look?"

"No."

"Fine. I want you to do something else for me anyway. But you need to have an open mind."

Suspicion reared up. "You must want this very bad to bring me biscotti."

"Stop—I brought the biscotti because I love you. But I want you to do this thing for me because I'm asking."

"Low blow. Tell me what it is first."

Gen pulled out a slim purple book from the paper bag. The cover was a thick, rich velvet, and the pages seemed worn. The scent of musty paper rose in the air. Izzy reached out and took it, stroking the beautiful cover.

The Book of Spells.

WTH?

Gen began talking fast, as if afraid if she got interrupted her sales pitch would fail. "I know you're going to think I'm crazy but I don't care. It's a book to create a love spell. For a man. Well, not just any man, but the man who is truly meant for you—your actual soul mate—and you need to follow the steps exactly as they're outlined, and then Earth Mother will send him to you. But you have to be extremely careful about the list. The list needs to contain qualities you need in a man, and you should be as specific as possible. Don't just write down anything. You need to take it seriously, because it's very powerful."

Izzy stared at the book, then back at her sister. A hum of energy seemed to rise in the room, settling in a thick haze around them. "Umm, Gen, I think you're working too hard."

Her sister's usual sense of humor didn't rise up to meet her teasing comment. "I'm serious, Izzy. I need you to do this. I know you don't believe me, but just humor me. The spell holds great power. I did it and now I'm with Wolfe. Arilyn and Kennedy and Kate also did the spell, and look at them. They're happy and in love with the men who are meant for them."

Izzy's mouth fell open. "You believe a love spell was the reason you hooked up with Wolfe? Babe, I hate to tell you this, but you two were circling each other for years. Even I knew you belonged together."

"It worked for all of us. I think the spell harnesses Earth Mother's energy and allows us to finally accept the love that is right for us."

"If Mom heard you talking like this, she'd kill you. She

always says you can't do voodoo and stuff and still be a Catholic."

"I'm still Catholic! But I believe in this. And you better not tell her."

Izzy shook her head in confusion, flipping through the pages. "Wait a minute. Arilyn mentioned Earth Mother in a conversation we had. Is this what she was talking about?"

"Yes. I told you, we all did the spell together. She mentioned to me I might want to pass the book on to you."

Damn, she had no idea everyone would go to such extremes just to get her a date.

She sighed. "This is weird, Gen. Why do you want to hook me up so bad with a guy? I'm finally happy and at peace. I'm not causing trouble, I'm off the drugs, and I'm happy. Why mess things up now?"

Gen reached across the counter and snagged Izzy's hand, squeezing. "Because I'm so proud of you and happy I have my sister back. Because you've done so much work, and grown, and changed, and I think you deserve a man who will treasure you in this life. Because I think you're worth a great love."

Emotion stung her eyes. Her twin's generous heart always amazed her. Years ago, her words would have made Izzy feel selfish and ashamed. As if Izzy were less because she didn't experience the same kindness as her twin. Those emotions would eventually turn to anger and then destruction. Because the truth was Izzy had never felt like a good person. She never felt like she was good enough to be Gen's twin.

But now, after therapy, Gen's words filled her with gratitude. She was lucky to have a sister who cared so much. "Ah
crap, don't make me cry!"

Gen sniffed. "Sorry. Just please promise you'll do it?
Pretty please with sugar on top?"

She swallowed back the lump in her throat. "And cher-
ries, too?"

"Yes."

"I'll do it."

Gen bounced in her seat with excitement. "Thank you!
Do you want to do it right now? I can help you."

Izzy laughed and threw up her hands. "No; right now
I'm tired and want to watch my movie and crash. I'll read it
this week. I don't know when I'll do it but I promise I will."

"Good enough for me." Gen got up, gave her a quick
hug, and headed out. "You'll be at Mom's house for Sunday
dinner, right?"

"I'll be there. Bye." She blew kisses at her sister and
locked the door behind her.

Izzy trudged back to the kitchen, put the plates in the
sink, and picked up the book. Her fingers tingled slightly.
She brought the book back to the couch, sat down, and
began to read.

MIDNIGHT.

Izzy stared at the ceiling. The witching hour. Or was that

3 a.m.? Did it even matter? She'd been tossing and turning for hours, unable to get the book out of her head. It was ridiculous and stupid. Yet it had given her an opportunity to really think about what type of man she'd not only want in her life but actually need.

The act of writing down intentions was powerful. She'd learned that from therapy and always kept a journal. But she'd never stopped long enough to analyze what she craved in a healthy relationship. It had always been about excitement and great sex and moving on.

Except that one night.

She pushed it to the back of her mind, got up, and walked into the kitchen. The book lay on the table. She turned on the light, grabbed her journal and pen, and began to write.

Her spirit soared a bit higher when she finished and read over the list. Yes. It seemed . . . right. Maybe this was enough for now—to actually know what traits to seek out. But she'd promised Gen she'd do the entire thing. She'd broken enough promises in her lifetime and had sworn to never do it again.

She read the directions carefully. Make two lists. Burn one and recite the prayer to Earth Mother. Put the other one under her mattress. That didn't seem so complicated. Still, she felt completely ridiculous doing a love spell for some random man out there.

With a sigh, she copied the list onto another sheet of

paper. Fishing around the cabinets, she took out a pot, grabbed her lighter, and opened the book to the right page. Saying a quick apology to her mother, she recited the prayer to Earth Mother and put the flame to the paper, dropping it into the pot and watching it burn.

Done.

Cleaning up the mess, she took the other sheet of paper and stuck it under her mattress. The book went onto her shelf, and she crawled back under the covers.

She wondered if Earth Mother held the power to send her Chris Hemsworth. Maybe that would finally banish Liam from her mind.

Then she fell straight into sleep.

three

$\mathcal{D}$EVINE STOPPED OUTSIDE the door. The silver-and-purple scrawl with sparkling white lights urged customers to step in. Too bad his feet felt like wet bricks stuck to the cement.

"It won't be bad," Stone said.

"You said I wouldn't have to go through this crap. You promised Arilyn would let me slide through without a hitch. You vowed you could handle her."

Stone sighed and rubbed his head. "I was wrong, okay? She's very stubborn when it comes to this love-match stuff. Said you had to have at least one introductory session and you needed to come in person to fill out the forms and talk with Kate. Hey, at least I got you out of makeover stuff with Kennedy!"

Devine turned to walk away, but Stone grabbed his arm, opened the door, and pushed him inside.

The office was cheery and welcoming, with more purple-and-silver decor. The waiting room had purple comfy couches, and more lights were strung around the walls with interesting artwork scattered about. The scent of vanilla hung in the air.

The front desk was empty.

"They're closed. Let's go."

"Don't be a pussy," Stone hissed. "She'll be right back. Here, I got a better way." He raised his voice. "Hey, Arilyn, are you back there? I got Devine!"

Devine closed his eyes. So fucking embarrassing.

Heels clicked in the hallway, and Arilyn came walking out with Pinky tucked under her arm. The moment the Chihuahua saw Stone, she began wriggling frantically. Stone met her halfway with his arms out. "There's my girl."

Arilyn handed over the pup, shaking her head as she watched Stone coo over her. "I thought I was your girl."

"You're both my girls. I'll show you my appreciation later."

"You better. Hi, Devine. How are you?"

"Good. Hey, I was thinking this isn't such a hot idea. We just came by to get Pinky for our afternoon run." Pinky had become a mascot at the police station and loved to ride in the squad car. With her crazy tufts of hair sticking up from her head, and ratlike face, he'd been afraid she'd be bait instead of a companion. But Devine had gotten just as attached to her as Stone and even began thinking about getting his own dog. Maybe that would help with this restlessness.

Stone snorted. "Ignore him. He's here to get the paperwork and sign up. He's ready."

Arilyn tilted her head, considering him with a probing green gaze. She had a stillness and grace to her that managed to completely balance Stone's roughness, making them an ideal match. "I know this is a big step, but you've already been out there, Devine. All we want to do is narrow the field to see if we can find a woman who fits you, but we can't do our job unless you sit down with Kate for an interview."

Devine shifted his weight. He could manage an interview. Maybe this wouldn't be as stressful as hooking up at the bar, or in line at the bakery, or in the secondhand bookstore. God knows he was running out of women in his demographic. "Okay. Maybe I'll try it."

Arilyn smiled. "Good. I'm going to give you some paperwork and schedule you a session with Kate."

The phones began ringing nonstop and Stone looked around. "Is Izzy here today?"

"She's just in the back to get some files."

"I'm here!" a husky voice called out. "Sorry, almost drowned in the back room. We really need to organize and clean that up, Arilyn. Maybe I can work on the weekend?"

"You work too much already."

"I don't mind. Hi, Stone, how are you?"

"Good. Hey, Izzy, I don't think you met my partner yet. He's been away on vacay. This is Devine."

Slowly, Devine turned his head and met her gaze.

The mess of files dropped from her fingers and hit the floor.

Isabella.

His body seemed to shut down organ by organ. Stillness fell over him as he gazed at the woman who had been haunting his dreams for the past six years. His one-night stand that had been so much more.

She was beautiful.

Her hair now held gorgeous, wild curls in a rich, deep brown. No more purple streaks. Those navy-blue eyes held a depth that had been missing before. A touch of regret and pain, but now there was a steely resolve, also shown in the tilt of her chin and the way she carried herself. Her petite frame had once been lean and sharp. Now she had gorgeous, full curves that made a man ache to touch her, be cradled within her softness. She wore flowy black pants that emphasized the flare of her hips, and a red T-shirt with a sequined heart. Just the hint of a thorny rose on her upper right breast peeked out, teasing him. Words stuck in his throat. He ached to cross the room and hold her. How was it possible that after all these years the connection still flamed and burned between them?

"Liam." The whisper of his name floated across the room. Her painted apple-red lips were full and ripe.

"'Liam'?" Stone looked back and forth between them, confusion evident. "Have you met before?"

They remained locked in place, staring at each other

with hungry eyes. "Yes. She knew me as Liam." When he enrolled in the academy, everyone began calling him Devine and it had stuck. "We met a long time ago."

He sensed Arilyn's fascination, but he still couldn't seem to speak anything intelligent. As if Pinky sensed the growing tension, she whined softly. Izzy seemed to jolt out of her spell, shaking her head as if to clear it. "I'm sorry; it was just a shock seeing you again. You look . . . well." She seemed to notice she had dropped the papers and scrambled to pick them back up.

"So do you."

She stood up again. More staring. Finally, Stone interrupted. "This is the weirdest meet I've witnessed in a long time. We have to get to our shift. Can you get Devine his papers, sweetheart?"

"Papers?" Izzy blurted out.

"Yes; we're signing Officer Devine up for Kinnections. Can you get me one of those packets, Izzy?"

"You're not married?" she asked.

He wondered if she'd taste the same. Whiskey hot and sugary sweet. Like maple syrup with a touch of bourbon. Intoxicating. "No. Are you?"

"No." She shook her head a second time, then dove for the desk, pulling out a bunch of stapled pieces of paper and handing them to Arilyn. "Here you go. That's the intake packet."

"Thanks," Arilyn said, handing him the papers. "Fill

these out and I'll get you an appointment with Kate next week."

He wished Izzy had handed him the papers. He would've been able to sneak in a touch and see if her skin was still super soft.

Stone kissed Arilyn and headed out with Pinky in his arms. "Bye, Izzy. Come on, team—let's catch some criminals."

He didn't want to go, and thought of what type of excuse he could use for lingering. But his brain had frozen up, so he just nodded like an idiot and followed his partner out the door.

Isabella was here.

LIAM WAS HERE.

A deep trembling shuddered through her body. Knees wobbling, she dropped into the chair behind her desk and tried to gain control. How was this possible? Six years. He looked the same, yet different. His hair was shorter, but the white-gold-streaked strands still reminded her of old Hollywood. Those thickly lashed, pale-blue eyes still stunned, but there were new lines carved in his face, adding a sexy roughness to his classical features. But his body . . .

Dear God, he filled out a cop uniform like a female fantasy on steroids. The dark blue fit him like a custom suit, emphasizing broad chest muscles and powerful thighs. When she'd first walked in, her gaze had been tattooed to his ass, even more droolworthy with the addition of a large leather belt with various items, including a holstered gun. His short-sleeve uniform revealed golden hair scattered down the tanned skin of his forearms. His shoes were polished to a high sheen, but it was the way he stood there, feet braced apart, hands propped on hips, as if he were about to arrest her and then do bad, naughty things to her body.

Her skin flushed at the image, and she gulped for air.

The memory of that night still haunted her. Had she ever experienced such a sensual, intimate encounter? Liam allowed her to connect on a level she never knew existed, and it changed her forever.

It was also the night she'd done the cocaine, and the start of the real downward slide her life became. It had made her feel like a goddess and indestructible. The next morning when she crashed, she got more. Before, she'd always kept a delicate balance, making sure she never took cocaine two days in a row. Suddenly, weed wasn't good enough anymore, and she craved another hit of coke. She needed bigger and better and stronger. She needed to forget Liam walking away from her in disgust.

So she did. And spent the next years spiraling toward disaster.

Despair hit. Had he pitied her? Regretted even sleeping with her? Her memories of him were sacred—a beautiful thing to pull out, dust off, and savor. But seeing him again ruined it all, because he'd been right. Drugs had ruined her, and he had been the one to see her take the first terrible step.

Her skin burned with humiliation.

"Izzy?"

She looked up at Arilyn. Her friend's face held a gentleness that soothed. "Were you two involved before?"

Slowly, she nodded. She'd never told anyone about Liam or that night. Not even Raven. But now she found the words spilling out. "We had a one-night stand. He was entering the police academy and asked me to see him again. I know we barely knew each other, but I said yes. He was different. There was a powerful connection."

Arilyn smiled. "Oh, do I know about those. Feeling close to another person can be the most wonderful thing in the world. Also the scariest."

"It was. And then I blew it."

"We've all made those mistakes. You were also very young."

"It was more than that," she whispered. "I chose drugs. I needed them more than him."

Arilyn squeezed her shoulder. "Yes. Sometimes we choose wrong. And then sometimes we get a second chance."

Izzy straightened up. Resolve leaked into her voice. "No. Liam and I were never meant to be together. He's a very different person than I am. I think Kinnections will help him find the perfect woman. Someone who's good."

"You're good, Izzy."

She forced a smile. "I know. But not for him."

The phone saved her from talking further. Arilyn frowned but slowly walked away.

He might be Stone's partner, but she didn't have to deal with him. He'd keep his distance, and she'd keep hers. She rarely had one-on-one meetings with clients, and maybe she'd explain to Kate it would be better for both of them if they stayed apart. Verily was a big town, and she was positive they wouldn't run into each other.

Izzy ignored the touch of sadness and threw herself into her work.

four

TWO DAYS LATER, Devine sat in the car and stared at the house.

This was crazy. He had no right to knock on her door and demand to talk to her. After all, they'd only shared a night of sex. Great sex. Sex that wrecked him and made him compare her to every other woman he'd slept with since. Still, it was unbelievable she would've remembered him so clearly the moment their gazes met. Could this be considered stalking? Harassment?

His damn palms were sweating.

He raked them down his jeans. The real problem was it was more than sex. He'd thought of her constantly over these past six years, her beautiful face haunting him in his dreams. How many times had he tortured himself about his decision to leave? If he would've stayed, could he have convinced her not to take the drugs? Would things have ended differently?

He didn't know. But now she was here in Verily, back in his life, and there was no way he'd miss this opportunity for a second chance.

It had been easy to find out where she lived. Stone had offered the information that she'd taken up residence in the bungalow when Arilyn moved in with Stone. He hadn't meant to drive over. Coming home from the pool hall, he just kind of found himself here and decided to park and think a bit.

In front of her place.

The light was still on, and the blinking colors told him she was watching television. Women hated being interrupted during their evening routine. If he knocked, she probably wouldn't even open the door. This was stupid.

He got out of the car.

He couldn't knock.

Cursing under his breath, he paced back and forth on her front porch, trying to psych himself up. Okay, so maybe she remembered him, but it didn't mean she'd been dreaming of him all these damn years. He was about to make a complete ass out of himself. Stone would eventually hear about it and torture him. But if he didn't talk to her, he'd regret it. If he was really going to try to find a woman through Kinnections, he needed to flush Isabella out of his system for good.

Right?

Devine didn't expect her to actually open the door to his knock. He waited for a while, shifting his feet, feeling like the schmuck he was for the slim opportunity she'd want to talk to him, too.

The door opened.

She wore gray sweatpants and an old, worn-out gray T-shirt. The soft, washed cotton molded to every curve. Her curly hair was pinned up on her head, but unruly strands escaped from every direction. No makeup. Bare feet. Toes painted purple.

His dick sprang to life and strangled within his jeans. The sizzle was immediate and just as intense as it was six years ago. Her dark-blue eyes widened to the size of saucers as she stared at him.

"What are you doing here?"

Good question. She'd always been direct. He cleared his throat. "I wanted to talk."

She blinked. "About what?"

A strangled laugh escaped his lips. His humiliation grew. "About us."

"There is no us."

"Isabella, can you please let me in just for a minute? Please?"

A frown creased her brow. She waited a few long moments, and Devine figured he'd be thrown off her porch to do a walk of shame minus the sex. Finally, she motioned him in with a jerk of her hand. He stepped inside and shut the door behind him.

She crossed her arms in front of her chest as if to protect herself. That hidden touch of vulnerability squeezed his heart. What was it about this woman that fascinated him? "I'm sorry I barged in on you like this. I just wanted to talk."

She shook her head. "About what? We slept together six years ago. I'm sure this stuff happens now and then. Just because you're Stone's partner doesn't mean we can't keep our distance."

For one moment, he wondered if he should just walk out the door. Maybe this had been a terrible idea and she really didn't want to see him again. But hell if he'd back off now when he needed to find his own answers. His frown matched hers. "Don't want to keep my distance. I've thought about you these past years. How are you doing?"

Ice chilled her eyes. He knew he had made a mistake from the way she squeezed herself tighter as if to ward off an attack. "Oh, I get it," she said softly. "You want to confirm all of your ideas about me came true. You want to know you made the right decision by walking away from me."

"Isabella—"

"No, I understand why you came here. Let me give you the short version. I took the coke after you left. Then I took more the next day. This continued with greater frequency, which you don't need to know, until I found myself without family, friends, or an ability to live. I finally checked into rehab, did my work, and now I'm clean and sober." She smiled tightly. "So you see, Liam, you were right about everything. Now that we've strolled down memory lane, I'd like you to leave."

"Fuck. I didn't mean—I'm not talking about that shit! I hate that it happened to you, but I'm not here to judge or gloat over being right. I didn't want to be right! I'm here because the woman I spent the night with was special, and I want to get to know her again."

Her muscles relaxed slightly. "That night was special to me, too," she said softly. "But there can't be anything between us anymore, Liam. We're too different." Her small laugh was humorless. "I knew it when I met you. You were heading toward greatness. You're a police officer, just like you dreamed. And you were right to warn me about the drugs, but I couldn't hear you then. I was too trapped within my own stuff."

"But you're clean now," he pointed out. "You faced your demons. I just want some time with you. Don't we owe ourselves that after the way we left things?"

"No. We owe ourselves the truth. We'd never be good together."

"You won't even give me a chance?"

Her eyes held not only a touch of sadness but a banked fire that snapped with ferocity. "I'm not even thirty years old and I don't feel comfortable in a bar. Or at a party where everyone's drinking. I go to meetings on a monthly basis, and I have a mentor I still regularly check in with. Every day, I wake up and tell myself I'm not going to drink or use. Every night, I almost weep with gratitude that I stayed clean. Is that the type of girlfriend you want? I have more baggage and issues than you could possibly imagine. You think that'll be fun for you?"

Her words pegged him like jagged glass splitting skin. The truth shone in her face, the acceptance of what she'd experienced and the new path she walked. She was right. He could have an easy woman, one who clung to his arm and accompanied him to social events, who drank beer with him while he played pool, who he never had to worry about or doubt.

Problem was, that woman wasn't Isabella. A woman he'd spent one too-short evening with. A woman whose last name he didn't even know.

His entire life had been about achieving goals and reasonable expectations. From his grades to mentoring his younger brother to making his parents proud. He was precise, controlled, and liked things neat. Police work called to his sense of justice and righting the imbalances of life.

But he'd found something else about himself throughout the years. People were messy. So was life. He'd arrested criminals who broke the letter of the law but who he could easily understand. They had difficult backgrounds. Made wrong choices. Screwed up. He'd realized imperfection had a rough beauty about it, especially when people held a willingness to see the truth about themselves.

Izzy had reached that type of epiphany that most never got to. She'd done it the hard way, but damned if he didn't want to delve deeper to see the woman she'd built through disaster.

So he gave the only answer he could. "Yes."

She tilted her head, regarding him. "Yes what?"

"Yes, I think it will be fun, because I'd get to be with you. Will you go out to dinner with me?"

She gulped, staring at him like he'd gone crazy. "No! I just told you all the reasons we're not good together."

He smiled slowly. "I don't think they're good reasons. Unless you're seeing someone?"

He caught the flash in her blue eyes. She wanted to lie, but she didn't. "No."

"Good. How about Friday night?"

"No, Liam. You have to go. I'm not going to date you or pursue this any further. Kinnections will find you a woman who's meant for you."

He analyzed the situation. He bristled at her determination to dismiss him before getting to really know him. He also understood her wariness. He needed to move slowly so she could get used to the idea of him being around. She needed to begin to trust he was interested in her, including her past. This brief encounter only proved the energy between them was real. They were connected in some way and needed to explore that deeper.

He also desperately wanted her in his bed.

Devine nodded. "Okay, I'll leave. But first you need to answer one question."

"What?"

"What's your last name?"

Her tentative smile was sweet and ripped at his heart. "MacKenzie. Isabella MacKenzie."

There was so much more he craved to know, but it would have to come later. "Isabella MacKenzie," he repeated, rolling the name on his tongue like a caress. "I like it."

"Should I be calling you Devine, instead?"

"Never. You can call me Liam. That's who I will always be with you."

She pressed her lips together. Then opened the door. "Good-bye, Liam."

He wanted to ruffle her hair or touch her cheek. Tell her not to worry. Instead, he kept his distance. "Good-bye, Isabella."

When he left, excitement and promise surged in his blood. Her honesty humbled him. She never flinched when she told him her story, owning her mistakes as well as her triumphs. She had been fascinating and confident when he'd first met her six years ago.

Now she was pure magnificence. Real.

And the challenge of a lifetime.

Driving away, he felt as if the color had leaked back into the world around him, ripe with the tantalizing fruit of the unknown. The strange restlessness inside quieted.

five

ZZY DRAGGED IN A BREATH and prepared herself for the upcoming hour.

She could handle it. Liam had an appointment with Kate for his interview so he'd be matched with the right woman. Kate was a genius when it came to her matchmaking skills, besides having a very special talent that Izzy had a hard time believing at first but finally witnessed in full force. When Kate put her hands on two people who were soul mates, she got jolted by an electrical shock. Gen had given her the entire story of how Kate had met her husband, Slade, when he stormed into Kinnections calling her a fraud. Izzy could only imagine how their love story had played out.

Arilyn and Kennedy were out of the office, and the day had been a bit calmer than usual for an early Wednesday afternoon. The lunch-hour rush had passed, so she kept busy working on the spreadsheets and calculating matching data to load back into the system to find proper matches.

She was still experiencing aftershocks from Liam's evening visit.

Knowing she'd been just as important to him that night had healed some deep wounds. But there was no way she could relive a night where she consistently questioned her actions, wondering if she had listened to Liam and climbed back into bed her path would've veered in a different direction, saving so many people she loved horrible pain.

Regrets are part of healing. You can never take back your actions, but you can forgive, make amends, and move on. You have a responsibility to lead a full, happy life, for you and God. Obsessing about regrets will poison your soul.

Her sponsor's words echoed in her mind, allowing her to calm down.

Her body thrilled to life when he told her he wanted to have dinner, but her brain firmly dragged her back from the precipice. She couldn't have sex with Liam. She was past jumping into bed with a guy because it scratched an itch, and though she couldn't regret her open sexuality, she'd changed. She realized she'd dove into sex as an escape from her real problems and swore the next time she got physical with a man, it would be because real feelings were there.

He may have offered dinner, but she knew the hidden meaning behind the words. He wanted her in bed, just like six years ago. Problem was, she was a different person now and he'd only be disappointed.

Her body raged and whined. Two years with no sex was

a damn long time. Especially when orgasms had been a regular occurrence. Now she had to rely on a machine, and although it was capable, it was definitely not the same.

On cue, Liam walked in.

Her hands fisted, then slowly relaxed. He was out of uniform, wearing dark-washed jeans, a pale-gray button-down shirt, and leather tied shoes. Even out of uniform he looked handsome. Proper. And sexy as hell.

He stopped in front of her desk and leaned over. Trying not to shrink back, she watched the color of his pale-blue eyes reflect a tinge of silver, hypnotizing her. His perfect face could have launched a thousand movie careers. "Hi, Isabella. I'm here for my appointment with Kate."

"Of course." She prayed her skin wasn't turning a hot pink. Why did she suddenly feel like a schoolgirl? She was always so confident in her sexuality. "Umm, Kate is running a bit late. Let me take you into the conference room so you're more comfortable while you wait."

"I'm comfortable hanging with you."

His easy smile curved full lips. She had a sudden urge to lean over and take a succulent bite. "No! I mean, you need to wait in there for her. It's more comfortable."

"So you said."

Damn him. Amusement laced his molasses-rich voice. She wasn't going to let him make her uncomfortable. "Follow me," she snapped smartly, getting up and leading him down the hall.

Her ass tingled like his gaze was stuck on it.

The room was large, set up for easy conversation and sharing. The silver rug was accented by purple chairs, a large mahogany desk, and encouraging signs scattered about the walls. A large coffee machine and pitcher of homemade lemonade sat on a side table. "Can I get you anything?"

"Yes."

"Coffee? Lemonade?"

"Have dinner with me."

She jerked slightly. "No, thank you. If you'll just take a seat, Kate will be right with you."

"It's just dinner."

Her brow arched. "Nothing is just dinner. If you haven't learned that yet, you've been with the wrong women."

He laughed. "This time it would be. I just want to talk."

"Said every man in the history of time. Excuse me."

She walked out with her head held high, breathing a sigh of relief when she was out of his energy force field. She'd never met another man who affected her like this. The phone rang, and she jumped to get it. "Kinnections matchmaking agency."

"Izzy? It's Kate. Listen, I have a huge problem and I need your help."

"Are you okay?"

"Yes, but I got a flat tire on my way and Slade insisted he come to get me even though I have Triple A. He says he doesn't trust them."

"I think it's sweet he's a bit overprotective."

Kate snorted. "Yeah. The only reason I'm letting him is he's been working late at the office this week and I haven't seen much of him. It will give us a quick opportunity to have a roadside drive-thru lunch."

"Romantic. Your appointment is here. I'll reschedule for you."

"No, I'll be able to get there in half an hour. I need you to do the initial intake for me. We've gone over it and you're ready. The papers are right on my desk, so complete the first two forms for me, and I can jump in for the rest."

Izzy's mouth dropped open. Kate never let anyone else interfere with her clients' first appointments. "I don't understand. Let me check with him—maybe he can wait till you get here."

"No, I have back-to-back appointments and I can't reschedule. It's critical, Izzy; I know you can do it. Just write down all of his answers. Make him feel comfortable. I'll get there as soon as I can."

Her heart pounded so hard the echo reached her ears. Her first shot at a client and it had to be Liam? Why was this happening to her? "Sure, no problem," she said with forced brightness. "I can handle it."

"Great—I knew you could! See you soon."

Izzy replaced the receiver, dropped her face in her hands, and groaned. How was she going to do this? The questions were intimate—and crucial to making the right match. But she didn't have the time to explain to Kate about their past relationship. She just had to be professional. She could handle this.

She headed to Kate's office to pick up his file, shuffled through the forms, and grabbed a few pens, then walked into the conference room.

"Kate has been slightly delayed," she said calmly. "She would like me to start the intake process, and then when she gets here, she'll take over. Unless this isn't acceptable to you. If not, I'd be happy to reschedule the appointment."

He was lounging in the violet cushioned chair, ankles crossed, head back in a relaxed pose, reminding her of a graceful cat taking a break between hunts. The pleased look on his face told her he was quite happy with her statement. "Fascinating—I didn't know you did any of the matchups."

She threw her shoulders back. "This is my first. Again, if you'd rather wait for Kate—"

"No. I want to be your first."

The words hummed with meaning and crackling sexual tension. She clung to her professional demeanor tighter than a politician to fake promises and sat down in the opposite chair. Cursing her luck that she wore a decently short skirt today, she gave a quick tug, then propped the folder on her lap. Clicking the pen, she paused on the first question.

"Tell me one of the reasons you want to find love now."

"I need a little foreplay first."

The pen dropped from her fingers and rolled to the floor. "Excuse me?"

He tamped down a grin, retrieved her pen, and held it out to her. She snatched it back, trying to make sure their fingers couldn't touch. "Foreplay. I'm not comfortable getting right into serious questions without some warm-up conversation."

She wanted to scream with frustration, but she wanted to impress Kate. Damn him. He was having fun with this and didn't seem the least bit stressed about her asking him intimate questions. "Conversation? Fine. How was your day?"

"I gave out two speeding tickets, dealt with one minor traffic accident, and gave out four Breathalyzer tests. I had the night shift, so I'm a bit worse for wear."

Yeah, right. He looked fresh, other than his hair being a bit mussed up. It only made him look hotter. "Did they all pass?"

"Yes." A smirk rested on his lips. "I had to give one to a father who was throwing up on a neighbor's lawn. She called the police, suspecting him of drunk driving. Turned out his toddler had vomited in his minivan and he's a sympathetic vomiter."

"Oh no. Bet his wife is going to hear about that."

"He was desperately texting her through the whole mess."

Izzy laughed and relaxed a bit. "So your job has many potential pitfalls."

"Yes, but a small-town cop doesn't see much action. Which is good, don't get me wrong. But sometimes—"

He cut himself off. She waited. When he didn't say anything else, she gave in to her curiosity. "Sometimes what?"

He shrugged. "Sometimes I wonder if there's more out there for me." Suddenly, his pale-blue eyes glinted with a fierce determination. "Which is why I'm here right now. I'm ready for more. Does that answer your question?"

Shivers raced down her spine. He had the oddest ability to be relaxed one moment, then intense the next. She remembered the way he'd casually leaned against the wall that first night they met, then closed the distance with a purpose that made her belly drop.

Professional . . . professional . . . professional . . .

"Yes, thank you." She scribbled down his answer in the white space. "What type of hobbies or interests do you currently pursue?"

"I dance."

Her head shot up. "What?"

"I dance. I'm not a stripper, though. Kind of like *Flash-dance*. But the pole gives me some issues."

The memory rose and exploded between them. God, had he remembered her every word? Caught between laughter and irritation, she shook her head and allowed a small smile. "Very funny."

"You never tried it again, did you?" he asked softly.

"Dancing? God, no. Didn't want to torture myself or others."

"Doubt a man alive could be tortured watching you dance for him."

Wicked heat licked through her body. Her nipples hardened through her lace bra, and her thighs clenched under her short skirt. Oh, this man was good. Ignoring his comment, she strove for a proper tone. "Sports? Gym? Hiking? Books? It's important to find the things you like to do and achieve a good balance with your partner."

"None of the above. Not too interested in any sports. I use the gym because I have to keep my body in shape for my job. I like to read but it's nothing I'd consider a true hobby." He paused as if trying to come up with something. "I like *Star Wars*."

Izzy froze. No way. Impossible. "What did you say?"

"You know the movies? *Star Wars*? Silly, but I'm kind of a junkie. Was obsessed when I was a kid, and with the new franchise, it just set me off again."

She stared at him, unable to speak.

"Umm, now that you're looking at me like I'm weird, I'd like to retract my statement."

"No, I'm sorry; it's just that I happen to really like *Star Wars*, too."

"You kidding me?"

"No. Because I'm a girl you don't think I can like it?"

He threw up his hands in defense. "No, you surprised me. Who's your favorite character?"

"Princess Leia. But Rey is kick-ass and comes in second. She's a tie with Yoda."

"Gotta love a woman in a gold lamé bikini who can fight."

"Why are men so obsessed with that bikini?"

"It's epic. If you ever wore one, they'd need to resuscitate me."

Why did he have to make her want to laugh? It was the worst torture. She fought her grin desperately. "Who's your favorite?"

"Han Solo." Surprise must have shown on her face. "You didn't peg me for a Solo and Chewie guy?"

"Solo is a rebel. Smuggler, criminal, smart-ass. I would've pinned you for a Luke fan. He's more the hero. The rule follower. In a good way, of course."

"Han is more interesting to me. More layers. More . . . passion."

The air lit and charged. She shifted her weight, tore her gaze away, and tried desperately to focus on business. Matching him with someone else. "What do you do when you're not working? Or on weekends?"

"Play pool. Tinker at my house. I bought a fixer-upper and I like to work on small projects. I enjoy seeing my friends and family. My job has been my main priority. I take extra shifts to help some guys out. Our department got cut, so we never have enough manpower."

Yes, he'd always struck her as responsible. He served others and didn't bitch about it. His low-key style only emphasized his goodness, because he didn't brag or try to be someone he wasn't. He reminded her of Gen.

"Do you love your job?" The question wasn't on the forms, but it had popped out. He'd never know.

"Yes. I was meant to be a cop; it's part of who I am. Last year, Stone and I closed down a dogfighting ring. That's where he got Pinky from—she was pretty battered up for a while. We also succeeded with a big drug bust that was crippling this town. So, yes, my work gives me satisfaction that I'm doing my part."

Shame flooded her. He'd been fighting to keep drugs off the street and she'd been a classic junkie. They were from two different worlds.

"Don't."

Izzy startled at the whiplash of his voice. "What?"

His gaze burned into hers. "You had a past. You've suffered for it. You're clean now and doing everything you can to stay that way one day at a time. Don't use it as an excuse to push me away."

She almost finished the session. His body heat practically pulled her in, tempting her to close the distance, slide onto his lap, and thrust her fingers into his glorious hair. Kiss his lips and savor the intoxicating taste of cinnamon and hot need. His words threw her off, but underneath was a deeper truth that told her he believed what he'd spoken. He didn't seem to judge or blame her for that night. For choosing the drugs.

But she could never forget.

"Maybe we should take a break," she managed huskily.

He leaned back in the chair, relaxing again. "No need. What else do you need to know?"

Relief loosened her muscles. Question three was easy. "Favorite color?"

He frowned and looked uncomfortable. "I don't want to answer that."

"Why? It's the easiest question on the form."

"I pass."

Oh, this was too intriguing. "You're refusing to tell me your favorite color? Really?"

He blew out an annoyed breath. "Fine. But remember, this stuff is confidential."

"Of course."

"Chartreuse. I like chartreuse." His ears turned a tinge of red, and Izzy was struck by the ridiculousness of the entire situation.

She burst into laughter.

"See? That's why I didn't tell you." But his face had softened, and pleasure shone from his eyes. "God, you're so damn beautiful when you laugh."

Her heart thundered and her palms sweat, and in that moment, she didn't know if she could resist him.

The door flew open.

"I'm here! I'm so sorry, Devine. I hope Izzy was able to make you comfortable while you were waiting."

His gaze never broke from Izzy's. "She took good care of me."

"Excellent." Kate smiled. "Thank you so much, Izzy."

"You're welcome." She stood up on shaky legs and handed her the file. "I made certain notes so you can take it from here. Good to see you, Devine."

His last name stumbled over her tongue, sounding strange. He frowned. "Liam," he said brusquely. "Call me Liam."

She nodded and fled.

Back at the safety of her desk, she closed her eyes and breathed deeply, finding her center. It was done. She'd proved she was capable to Kate, and hopefully she wouldn't have to see Liam again. He'd be put through a series of social events or his profile would be run through their matching system to begin setting up dates. He'd find the right one through Kinnections. She knew it.

Izzy focused on work, trying not to check the time to see how long they'd been in there, when Kate finally walked out. Kate's voice rose in the background. "It was good seeing you, Devine. I have the information I need, and I'll be in touch to let you know if, well, if your certain requirements have been met."

"I appreciate it."

Izzy was staring at the computer but felt the exact moment he stood by her desk. His body heat practically lashed at her, urging her to look at him. "Thanks for your time, Isabella."

She shivered but forced herself to meet his gaze. "You're

welcome," she said. "I'm sure you'll be very satisfied with Kinnections."

"I'm sure I will be."

The statement sounded like a threat. Kate moved toward them with a thoughtful look, handing Izzy some papers. "Can you file these for me, please?" Kate stood next to Devine and patted him on the shoulder. "Tell Stone I said hello."

"Will do."

Izzy reached over to grab the files from Kate's hand, their fingers brushing.

In a flash, Kate stumbled back with a shocked look on her face, twisted away, and crashed to the floor.

Izzy jumped up and Liam knelt down to reach for Kate's hand. "Kate, are you okay?"

Kate threw her hands up in a frantic gesture and jumped to her feet. "Fine! I'm sorry; I j-j-j-just turned wrong and f-f-f-fell."

"Are you sure?" Izzy asked, trying to approach her.

Her boss glanced back and forth between Izzy and Liam, taking another step back. "Just embarrassed! Really, I'm fine. Umm, bye, Devine."

Her pointed dismissal puzzled Izzy, but Devine just nodded and headed out. "Thanks again, ladies."

He shut the door and the bell overhead tinkled merrily.

Kate stared at his retreating back, cradling her hand as if it were injured. Her face reflected an odd wonder. "You're freaking me out," Izzy said. "Are you sure you're not hurt?"

"Yes, I'm fine. I apologize. I need to talk to you about something important."

"Sure. Tell me what you need."

"I had a very interesting exchange with Devine."

Izzy frowned. "He wasn't happy with the intake I did?"

"Oh, no, nothing like that. Quite the opposite. It seems you charmed him so completely, he decided he doesn't want to join Kinnections until one of his requests is met."

"What request?"

Kate tapped her finger against her lips, pausing for a long moment. A sense of premonition crashed over Izzy, telling her something was about to change. "He said he can't move on with a clear heart until he takes you to dinner."

Her mouth dropped open. *"What?"*

"Now, normally I wouldn't even consider such a request. But he explained how he thinks about you a lot and wants the opportunity to have some time with you so he can begin his journey for love with a clear-minded focus. Seems he believes one dinner date will give him the time to settle some unresolved feelings toward you. I had no idea you both had met before, Izzy."

She tried to yell but a tiny squeak escaped her lips. She tried again. "That's ridiculous! We had a brief encounter six years ago and haven't seen each other since. I knew him as Liam, not Devine, so I never made the connection. I was going to tell you, Kate, but I felt like I could handle it."

"You did nothing wrong. I'm sorry I put you in that position. And I'm certainly not going to force you to go to dinner with the man if you're not interested." She narrowed her gaze thoughtfully. "Are you interested?"

Izzy groaned and rubbed her temples. "It doesn't matter if I'm interested. We're not meant for each other."

"You sure?"

"Positive. We're two very different people."

"I thought the same exact thing about Slade and me. Until we got to know each other better and realized we were the perfect match."

"I'm not you."

Kate's voice softened. "No, you're not. You have your own journey to complete. Why don't you take some time to think about it? It's just dinner. If you could both close some of those open doors haunting you, maybe this is a good thing."

In that moment, Izzy realized Kate wanted her to go. There was an odd urging in her eyes, as if she was trying to relate how important it was for Izzy to confront her past. If she did this, Liam might realize how they could never work, and embrace what Kate could do for him at Kinnections. Was she being selfish by not agreeing to have a simple dinner?

Nothing was simple, especially a dinner. She'd meant it when she said that to him, because the dynamics between a man and a woman were always complicated.

But she could keep it simple. If she focused and concentrated on proving her point, maybe she could find her own peace.

"Just think about it, Izzy. I have to do some work before my next appointment. Will you be okay?"

She smiled. "Yes, thanks. I'll think about it."

Kate walked down the hall, leaving Izzy to her thoughts and the haunting image of Liam's pale-blue eyes.

Six

SHE'D MADE A HUGE MISTAKE.

Izzy paced back and forth and wondered if it was too late to cancel. She tried meeting him at the restaurant, but Liam was insistent that he pick her up. Her original plan was to wear something casual and not think too much about it.

Four hours later, every piece of clothing and all shoes had been thrown around her bedroom in a panic. She used to be trendy. Her wardrobe reflected a cool free spirit who owned her sexuality. A bit of a badass, she liked showing off her tats and her piercings and displaying her body.

Now most of the stuff was yoga pants, comfortable T-shirts, and flats. She'd removed all of her piercings a while ago. Her feet practically curled up to try to hide when she stuffed them into a pair of her old stilettos. When had this happened to her? How had she become such a drab woman?

Yes, her recovery had taken long, hard work and she'd needed to make changes. But was this going too far? Had she lost some of her true essence in her fear to never relapse?

She'd finally settled on sleek black pants tailored to accent all her curves. The violet shirt was an upscale halter top with a sheer back and a crisscross of lace in the front. It was sexy but tasteful. She left her hair loose, donning silver chandelier earrings, lots of bangles that clinked when she moved, and a chain-link ankle bracelet with a small silver skull. Her black platforms were high but had a solid blocked heel. She'd kept her purple polish on her finger- and toenails, and used glittery purple eye shadow to emphasize her cat-eye liner.

She was ready.

But she wanted to cancel. Why oh why had she agreed to this?

The bell rang.

Cursing under her breath, she threw back her shoulders, marched to the door, and flung it open.

Blinked. Oh my. She was in trouble.

Liam Devine was divine.

He wore a suit. The black material clung to all the right places, emphasizing the breadth of his shoulders, the bulge of his biceps, the lean length of his legs. His dress shirt was a gray pinstripe, opened at the neck for a more casual look. The fact he wasn't wearing a tie was dead sexy, making her imagine how easy it would be to pull those buttons open and feast. Her gaze fastened on the strip of skin covered in golden hair her hands ached to reach out and touch. His halo-like hair gleamed even in the dim light, and his square jaw was cleanly shaven. Some delicious woodsy cologne drifted to her nostrils and made her want to paw at the ground like a bitch in heat.

His voice came out in a low growl. "You look edible. Amazing. I'm a grown man and feel like I'm picking up my date for the prom."

She laughed, the tension easing away. "Me, too. Thanks. You look . . . really good."

"Thanks." He offered his hand in an old-fashioned gesture. She took it. "Our carriage awaits."

"It's not the squad car, is it?"

"Why? You got some cop fantasy I can help you out with?"

His wicked humor was unexpected but he made her laugh again. "I always wanted to turn on the flashing lights."

"That's an easy fantasy to fulfill. I was hoping for something more interesting."

"Not gonna happen."

"A man's gotta try." He opened the door to a white Ford Explorer. She slid in and smiled at the clean-car smell. Obviously, he kept his vehicle spotless, giving her an indication he cared for his belongings. He got in, started the car, and pulled away from the curb.

"Where are we going?"

"Though I love Cosmos and Mugs, I thought we'd try that new sushi place. Unless you don't like Japanese?"

"No, I love it. Sounds good." Silence settled over the car.

Izzy shifted her weight. Glanced out the window. Her tummy was back to its tumbling self. Sitting so close to Liam was making tingles shoot through her nerve endings.

"Izzy?"

"Yes?"

He glanced at her. "Thank you for saying yes."

She smiled. "Didn't give me much choice, did you? I have to give you kudos for creativity. And persistence."

"I know I pushed but you came back into my life and I need to know some things."

He needed closure. Of course. Maybe this wasn't about a big seduction game after all, and it was a simple way to let the memory of what could have been go. For both of them.

She ignored the disappointment and nodded. "Of course. I understand."

"Probably not. But you will."

She ignored the odd warning, lapsing into a more comfortable silence as they made the short drive to the restaurant. He parked and escorted her out. Main Street was full of activity due to the mild weather in early fall. Couples strolled arm in arm, dogs trotted on leashes, and cafés were jammed with activity. The slightly crooked pavement and cheerful white lights strung on the lampposts gave Verily a unique character she'd grown to truly love. Somehow, some-way, this had become her home.

They passed a few art exhibits and the long line for the ice cream shop and bakery. She enjoyed the relaxed walk, the breeze tugging at her hair, the sound of club music drifting from Mugs, until they came to the Sushi House. Red paper lanterns, a fire pit, and bright lipstick-red doors welcomed them in.

They were seated at their table in a quiet corner overlooking an elaborate fountain and a Japanese garden. Water trickled from a serene Buddha over smooth, fat rocks, and cherry blossoms interweaved between latticed walls, adding charm. The waitress appeared, dressed in a bright-pink kimono, greeted them, poured tea, and silently disappeared.

"I love this already," she admitted. "Japan has always been on my bucket list but I never got there."

"Me, too. The culture fascinates me. *Shōgun* is my favorite book."

She laughed. His answering smile filled her with a deep joy she didn't want to analyze. It was the last time they'd be together. Maybe she should relax and enjoy his presence.

When the waitress asked for their drink order, she noticed Liam ordered a Coke. She ordered her usual cranberry and seltzer, then waited till they were alone again.

"You can order alcohol," she said quietly. "It doesn't bother me at dinner. I try to avoid wild parties but can handle a simple meal."

He considered her, steepling his elegant fingers together. "I ordered a Coke because that's what I wanted. I like to drink beer at the pool hall when I hang out with the guys from the station. Other than that, I'm not a big drinker. Never have been."

His words rang with the truth. Liam wasn't a liar. It was reflected in his intense blue eyes, deliberate actions, and quiet core. He knew who he was and didn't need to apologize. She'd known that when they first met.

"Okay."

"Okay. But please let's not say that word to each other again. I refuse to be cast in a sappy John Green movie that makes chicks cry."

Her lip twitched. "Hmm, so you saw *The Fault in Our Stars*, huh?"

"Absolutely not. The line is always posted on Facebook."

This time, the grin escaped. "I had no idea you had such a sense of humor."

"I didn't get a chance to show you." The waitress took their appetizer and dinner orders, then drifted away. "Tell me how you came to be working at Kinnections."

"I have a twin sister, Genevieve."

"Wait!" He shook his head as if trying to clear it. "Genevieve. Of course. I'm such an idiot. The first time I laid eyes on your sister, I saw you. Told myself it was my crazy imagination but now it all makes sense. Your face is the same. It's the other stuff that threw me off."

"Yes. When I turned eighteen, I hated how much we looked alike. It wasn't fun anymore; I wanted to be my own person. I dyed my hair, got my tats, some piercings, changed my wardrobe, and did everything possible to claim my own identity."

"Sorry, I'm still reeling that I never put it together. Go on."

"Gen worked at Kinnections when she left the hospital during a difficult time with her ex. I'd been on the outs with my family for years but had gone into rehab, done some work, and was getting stronger. We began repairing our relationship." A humorless laugh escaped her lips. "I hurt my sister terribly, but she welcomed me back without hesitation."

"She loves you."

The simple words struck home. "Yes. Gen is special. She belongs in the hospital helping others. Fortunately, she escaped the dickhead ex, moved in with Wolfe, who she'd always been in love with, and went back to surgery. Since Arilyn was living with Stone, the bungalow was free, and I was able to rent it. Eventually they had a spot open at Kinnections and hired me. It's only been a month but I'm very happy there. I may have found my niche."

"A closet romantic?" he teased.

"Maybe. Maybe I just like seeing the hope of a fresh start."

A surge of energy caught her like a sucker punch. Fortunately, the waitress glided back with their sushi rolls and miso soup, giving her a chance to breathe. She directed the conversation back to neutral topics. "Tell me about the academy and how you began work in Verily."

He used his chopsticks with expert ease as he popped a salmon roll into his mouth. Those long, tapered fingers moved with grace and purpose, reminding her of what they felt like on her bare skin. Strong teeth flashed, reminding her of how he'd bitten into the sensitive line where neck met shoulder. She remembered how much she liked it, that surprise sting she never saw coming.

Izzy cleared her throat and concentrated on her soup.

"The academy was a bitch, but I savored every moment. Learned a lot. Met some amazing guys who became good friends. I was assigned to Verily right from the start, and it was a good fit. Got myself a beautiful town and a nice house. I had a decent partner before Stone, but he wasn't as sharp or entertaining."

"The two of you are close?"

"Yeah. Not that we talk about it much, but I'd do any- thing for Stone. He came a long way and he's one of the best cops I've met."

"I bet it's important to have a partner you trust. A spe- cial bond."

"Yeah, especially since you spend more time than normal together. Kind of like a work marriage. A gay work marriage."

She laughed. Forking up a salmon piece, she swirled it in the soy sauce and ate. His brow shot up. "Why aren't you using chopsticks?"

"'Cause I suck at them. Like dancing. I have a problem with coordination."

"Not in every activity."

She shot him a suspicious look for the innuendo, but he looked innocent enough. Damn, he was whip smart. She relished the delicious banter and humming sexual tension. It had been so long since she'd felt so . . . alive. "What happened to your brother who attended college?"

"Got married. I took a week off for vacation and stayed with Matt for a bit. He's disgustingly happy and working as an advertising executive."

"You worried about him?"

"Hell, yes. He was the wild child in the bunch. Made fun of me a lot for being a dull stick-in-the-mud. Mom was a wreck there for a while, but eventually he found his way. I'm proud of him."

A deep longing washed over her. How wonderful his brother had ended up safe. She bet Liam beat his ass and watched over him. Still, Izzy knew by personal experience family sometimes could make no difference. The MacKenzie clan were well known to be tight-knit, supportive, and loving. They'd done nothing to deserve her wrath or rebellion—the demons had been lodged inside her a long time. She pushed away the thought. "Do you have any other siblings?"

"Nope, just us. I'm four years older than him, though, so I got to tell him what to do a lot. It was fun."

"I bet it was. Practiced being an officer of the law early, huh?"

He flashed a grin. His right tooth was still chipped. "Let's just say I got into a bit of trouble that time I handcuffed him in the basement and forgot he was down there."

She winced. "Damn, you're mean."

"Sometimes. My punishment fit the crime, though. My mother takes no crap from anyone."

"Sounds like *my* mom."

The waitress cleared the table and brought out sizzling plates of teriyaki shrimp and chicken, coconut rice, and steamed ginger vegetables, all sprinkled with sesame seeds. She held her fork with anticipation and dug in.

"Tell me about your family."

"They're kind of amazing. Big Italian family. I have my twin, my older sister, Alexa, and my brother, Lance."

"Are they married? Kids?"

She smiled, thinking of her crew. "Yes. Lance and Gina gifted me with my thirteen-year-old niece, Taylor. Alexa and Nick gave me two more nieces, Lily and Maria, who are nine and seven. Not to mention my two canine nephews, Old Yeller and Simba. Plus my Mom and Dad."

He shook his head. "I love it. Do they all live close enough to get together?"

"Yes; they live in New Paltz, so it's not a long drive for me. We still do family dinners on Sundays. Things get crazy."

"I bet. I always wanted a big family."

She stiffened at the twinge of pain. And he would. With some other woman. Izzy wanted to kill her already and he hadn't even had his first date with Kinnections. "It's good most of the time. Other times, it was challenging."

He paused from eating and speared her with his gaze. "Was your family a reason you turned to drugs?" he asked.

His direct question was honest and real. She hated when people acted embarrassed about her past, or spoke to her gently, as if she were fragile glass ready to shatter. They worried that she'd slide into some weird depression or burst into anger from talking about her drug habit. She gave back as much honesty as he could take and knew it would only help solidify their innate differences. "Not at all. There was some trouble with my parents for a while. My dad is an alcoholic. He took off and left us for a year, and everything fell apart. But he got sober, came back to prove himself, and Mom eventually forgave him. I had some daddy issues for a while, but he's not the reason, Liam. There is only one reason I turned to drugs. Myself."

He leaned forward, not releasing her from his stare. "What do you mean?"

"It's hard to describe. It was almost like something was . . . broken inside of me. I had this yawning emptiness and a constant restlessness that urged me to push things. I lived on the edge, trying all the time to make myself feel better. At first, sex helped. Being bad helped. I loved any type of adrenaline high or danger because it gave me a rush yet also gave me a calm I couldn't seem to find elsewhere. After high school, I decided to forgo college to travel, and that helped soothe the demons for a while. But they were always there, almost like a constant hum in my head. I started smoking weed and found it extended my peaceful time. No humming, just a glorious stillness. It made me happy."

She paused, but he reached across the table and snagged her hand. The slight tingle from his touch lit up her arm, but his hand was warm, and strong, and comforting, so she held it. "Go on," he said quietly.

"Then I found coke. And it was so much better than weed. I became everything I'd always wanted. Fulfilled. Happy. Strong and powerful. I was like a goddess reborn on that stuff. So I kept wanting more, but then my best friend, Raven, began to worry. She wanted me to avoid the coke and began watching me more closely. I began to sneak it in. I lied to her. I said bad things to hurt her so I could be alone and get high. I drank in between the highs and always needed more money to buy stuff. I hung out with the party crowd, though, so there seemed to always be something I could snort for free."

Oh, how she remembered that time in her life so vividly. When every object was sharp and overly bright. How she began losing herself and caring less and less about the people around her. How she cared less and less about the consequences of her actions that began to cause pain.

"What happened then?"

"It got bad. I got lost. Raven tried desperately to get me into rehab. I ended up leaving to go back to my family's house, and tried living there for a while, but they knew I was using. I was mean, real mean. At one epic family dinner, I came coked up and began screaming in front of my nieces, and my father finally threw me out of the house. Told me I was not welcome until I got clean."

"Where'd you go?"

She gave a half shrug, but the memories struck. "Everywhere. Anywhere. I crashed at friends' houses, slept in my car, haunted college campuses where I knew the pickings were good. Then one morning I woke up completely naked on some side road. My clothes were strewn everywhere. I have no idea if I had sex with one person or many. I didn't remember a damn thing. And you know what my first thought was?"

"What?"

"When I could get more cocaine." She pressed her lips together and shook her head. "And that's when I realized what had happened to me. I was nobody. Just some naked junkie dumped on the side of the road. I'd done that to myself. I got dressed, went inside, and called Raven. She came and got me, drove me straight to rehab, and I checked in. It was a long haul, but I feel good about my life now. But it's not a life that's easy." She eased her hand away and forced a smile. "That's what happened after you left. And now you can understand why this won't go beyond dinner."

He was quiet for a while. Izzy knew he was sifting through her words, trying to find the polite way to be supportive yet back away from his initial vow of pursuit. Dinner had served its purpose. Maybe he wanted to cut the night short and leave. She wouldn't blame him. So she waited for his decision.

"It only proves one thing to me, Isabella. You failed as spectacularly as you lived. You don't do anything half-assed. You own an inner strength that's as fierce as a tigress's. And you're not only a fascinating woman, you're real, honest, and not afraid to face your mistakes head-on. To me, that's someone I not only want to have dinner with but want to know on a much deeper level."

Her eyes widened.

"Since I have a feeling my admission freaked you out, I think we should talk about that another time. For now, let's enjoy our food. Have you ever tried fried ice cream?"

"What?"

"Fried ice cream. I've heard it's their specialty here, very decadent. Make sure you leave room for dessert. Now let me tell you a funny story about this bust Stone and I did that turned into a comic cluster."

He launched into a vivid retelling of his experience, seemingly done with their serious conversation. Shocked at his response to her confession, Izzy picked up her fork again. Her thoughts spun wildly, but she concentrated on his words and began eating.

HE WANTED ISABELLA MACKENZIE.

Bad.

Devine watched her posture relax as she began to realize the serious side of their conversation was officially over and he hadn't run out the door. Now that her shields had been lowered, he enjoyed watching the mischievous light in her dark-blue eyes when she teased him, and the easy laughter that burst from her lush red lips. Every nugget of knowledge she shared about her life was stored like a nut for winter within his mind. This woman made him feel more alive than anyone before, and he wasn't about to let her slip away. His entire dating history was bursting with a stream of women who had all been eager to take their relationship to the next level. There was nothing wrong with any of them. And each time he tried to push himself to settle in, compromise, be a father and husband as he'd always longed to be, something inside stopped him.

Because nothing was right.

His inner core yearned for something more. Years spent searching yet not finding. Because he'd already found it six years ago. In a college dorm room with a lost young woman who'd stolen his damn heart within a few dark hours.

Stupid. Ridiculous. He didn't work like this, and his feelings contradicted everything he'd once believed about himself. Devine believed in logic, not one-night stands that turned into love. But when he'd seen her again, it all fell into place for the second time. She fit.

Was it love? Impossible. Right? Lust would be acceptable, but he didn't just ache for her body. He ached to hold her gently, stroke her hair, comfort her. He longed to talk for hours, telling her everything he'd never shared with anyone. He imagined spending evenings together, holding hands, watching TV, doing all the daily tasks couples embarked on in a relationship.

But that would make her run. He needed to move slowly so she didn't spook. His plan was quite simple: do everything in his power to spend as much time with her as possible until she became used to him without realizing it. The problem was Kinnections. He certainly didn't want to be hooked up with another random woman at this point, but it was a gateway into seeing more of Isabella. He'd work on it.

They feasted on dessert, and he enticed her to take a stroll down Main Street. The crowds were winding down, and lone couples sat under umbrellas, sipping their last cappuccinos or eating ice cream, trying to squeeze the last ounce out of a warm fall evening. "I think I'm going to get a dog," Izzy announced.

He stopped and stared at her. "You're kidding me. I swear I just told Stone that I was ready to adopt a dog myself."

"Really?"

"Yeah. My house has a great yard. Every time I go out

there to rake leaves or do random cleanup, I feel like it's wasted. Would be nice to share my time with a dog."

They resumed walking. As their hands swung, their fingers brushed. "Arilyn mentioned taking me to her shelter. It's nice that she encourages animals in her bungalow. Most apartments don't allow it."

"You have a favorite breed? Big? Little?"

A smile lit her face. "Don't really care. I want one who speaks to me. My family has always had dogs, and my sister Alexa is a lot like Arilyn, very involved in the local shelters."

"Yeah, I don't do too much charity work. Kind of embarrassing. Work just fills up all the corners."

"I've been thinking of volunteering at one of the narcotics groups for teens. My mentor said she thinks I could be a big help just by sharing. I'm not sure if I'll be any good at it."

"You will. You'd relate well to teens. There's no bullshit with you."

Her laugh, husky and thick like honey, rose in the air and stroked his ears. His dick thickened. "Maybe you're right. I used to fear nothing. Once I got sober, I realized I was afraid of everything. Stupid, right?"

Devine couldn't help himself—there was no way not to touch her. He made the leap and intertwined his fingers with hers. His soul sighed. "'Courage is resistance to fear, mastery of fear, not absence of fear,'" he quoted.

A frown ruffled her brow. "Damn. Umm, Roosevelt."

"Nope."

"Wait! Mark Twain!"

"And how are you not a college graduate?" he teased.

"I swear I'm not a huge reader, but I like quotes. Stories about people who overcame odds or used their fame for good."

"That's reading."

She laughed again. "Yeah, I guess it is."

They walked the rest of the way back, hands clasped, enjoying the still, starry night, caught in a moment Devine knew he would always remember. When they returned to the car, he opened her door and drove back to her cottage.

The air changed between them, charging up like a battery gone haywire. His fingers clenched the steering wheel with each passing mile, as he didn't know how to break the climbing tension. He pulled over to the curb and turned to her.

"I had a really nice time."

She refused to look at him, fiddling with her seat belt. "Yes, me, too. Thanks for dinner. I better go."

She flew out of the car.

Cursing under his breath, he climbed out and followed her. When he reached the top step, her odd fear had leaked away and been replaced by the fierce determination he adored. "Look, it was a great night but we made a deal. I don't need you escorting me to the door, or making moony eyes and pretending this is going to be something it's not."

Navy-blue eyes burned with temper. His dick wept and it was all he could do not to back her against the door and kiss her savagely. "I don't make moony eyes at anyone. I take offense to that remark."

"Good night, Liam."

He moved into her space. "Are you attracted to me?"

The air escaped her lungs in a soft whoosh. His gaze flicked down her body, noting her tightening nipples against the fine lace of her bodice. She was practically shaking, and they hadn't even touched yet. "That's a ridiculous question."

"No it's not. Are you attracted to me?" She shifted her weight, struggling for the answer. "If you're not, I'll leave. I'm not out to force myself on anyone. But don't lie."

"I don't lie!" she said hotly.

"Are you?"

"Yes! But I don't intend to do a thing about it. This experiment is over, Liam. You need to finish what you started at Kinnections and we need to avoid each other. You deserve a woman who can be a perfect wife. You deserve kids and a white picket fence and dogs. You deserve it all."

He leaned in. "So do you," he growled. "Maybe it's time I prove it."

Shock and arousal dilated her pupils. Her lips parted for air. "I'm not out for a quick screw," she shot out. "Just because we did it once doesn't mean I'm an easy target."

"Sweetheart, you couldn't be easy if you tried. I knew

even that night you were the one who chose, not the other way around."

Her arms lifted as if to touch him, then dropped back down as if she'd gotten burned. The intoxicating scent of her invaded his nostrils: sweet and spicy, tinged with feminine arousal. He'd allowed her to lead because she needed to feel in charge, but he also knew when actions spoke louder than words. In his job, and his life, Devine followed an instinct that had never guided him wrong—an innate sense of when to push and when to back off.

Right now, he needed to push.

He moved.

It only took three steps to back her against the screen door. His arms caged her in. He braced his thighs apart, trapping her. He kept just enough space between their bodies so she had the time needed to transition without trying to bolt.

"I'm honored you feel the need to push me straight into another woman's perfect arms, but I'm here to tell you there is no perfect woman. And I'm sure as hell not perfect either. So, here's the deal, Isabella. I'm going to kiss you."

"What?" she squeaked out. She pushed against his chest briefly, then rested her palms over his beating heart. The move alone told him she wanted this as badly as he did. "We can't."

"We can. I haven't forgotten that night. Ever. It was the best damn sex I ever had. Even then, I wanted more, but it wasn't our time."

"Liam."

His name spilled from her lips in a sultry whisper, dissipating high above the stars. "Don't think. Don't worry." He lowered his head with deliberate slowness, wanting to savor every second. "Just kiss me."

His lips covered hers.

The years melted away. Her soft mouth trembled, then opened beneath his. He swallowed her groan and slipped inside, drinking in the sweet sting of her flavor, reminding him again of bourbon laced with maple syrup. They learned each other all over again until the kiss caught fire, and she sunk her teeth into his bottom lip.

A primitive growl rose from his throat and he rose to the demand. Twisting his fingers in her glorious hair, he pinned her open under the length of his thigh and ravaged her. His teeth nipped; he soothed with his tongue, claimed her as his.

She gave it back, sinking into a wild thing who exploded in his arms, challenging him at every turn. They feasted on each other, with a touch of the savage, her fingernails digging into the muscles of his arms, her breasts pressed tightly against his chest, her body arched with a demand he intended to serve. He got lost, got found, and fell hard within that one perfect, soul-stirring kiss.

Head spinning, breathing hard, he pulled away inch by inch. His dick screamed to take advantage of the moment, back her into the house, and take her now before she protested. But that wasn't what he wanted. When he got Isabella into his bed, she'd be damned sure she wanted to be there wholeheartedly.

Her eyes were glazed, her lips swollen and moist. He fought against the primal flood of arousal and clawed for control. "Liam?" His name was a beautiful question, and an answer he needed her to get used to.

"I want you." She shuddered in response. He bent toward her, forehead pressing against hers, hand cupping her cheek. "I want to strip off these clothes, touch and taste every inch of your skin, feel you come against my lips. I want to swallow you whole, make you scream, and do it again and again. Do you understand, Isabella?"

"Yes," she whispered. "I don't know if I can do this."

"You can. You just need time to get used to the idea."

She shook her head, pulling away, and Devine knew he'd lost her again. "Don't start something that's going to cause both of us too much pain. Please."

Her broken plea tore at his heart, shredding his insides. He lifted his hand in the air. "Sweetheart—"

"Good night, Liam."

She turned from him and disappeared inside, leaving him alone on her porch. He stood there for a while, caught between pushing her now and giving her some space.

Better to retreat and prepare the second phase of attack.

seven

A COUPLE DAYS LATER, Izzy pulled into the Animals Alive shelter with a sense of purpose and excitement. Liam's kiss haunted her.

She'd hoped if he ever kissed her again, the reality would never match the misty memory of that special night. Instead, the touch of his lips on hers shattered the past forever. Her body practically melted against him, helpless against his hot demand to surrender.

And, Lord, had she surrendered.

He'd grown into a powerful figure who not only challenged her mentally but brought a fierce masculine power that broke through all her barriers. She ached for him, and if he hadn't stopped the kiss, she would've allowed him to take her right against the door, like the animal he made her.

She was going to break her damn vibrator.

When Izzy went back to work, she worried he'd try to call, or show up, and she'd have to be harsh. She couldn't let a perfect kiss trick her into believing it could work for the long term. A cop and a former drug addict?

Impossible.

She already knew if she couldn't have Liam for more than a few nights, she'd rather rip off the Band-Aid now. Much easier to deal with a sharp pain than a slow-healing, raw wound.

Kate didn't push her for information on the date. Izzy hoped he'd honor their bargain, move on, and they'd do their best to avoid each other. After all, what man on earth would keep pursuing her? She'd turn him down every time, sometimes adding a bit of sting to help emphasize her point. She'd slammed the door on him after their date. Kind of. She knew men liked challenges, but Liam didn't play those games. Right?

After a long call with Meredith, her mentor, she felt more in control. Her mentor refused to interfere by advising but took a more subtle approach, allowing Izzy to talk freely and come to her own decisions. By the end of the conversation, Izzy decided to stay the course. It made the most sense.

So she decided she wanted a dog. Fast.

Arilyn practically danced with joy when she heard, then competently took over. They were meeting today to visit with the animals and see if she bonded. There was one thing she decided to stay away from. Puppies. She'd heard enough stories and seen Alexa's pain when her house got ripped apart and peed on, and when every designer shoe got eaten. She pictured a trained dog, still young, who'd be her loving companion, confidant, and sleeping partner.

She really needed someone in her bed, even if it was a canine.

"I'm so excited!" Arilyn said, giving her a hug when she climbed out of her car. The shelter was quite large, with outside runs for the dogs and a large, dark-shingled house off to the right. Farm animals grazed by the giant red barn, and acres of woods lay toward the back.

"Me, too. Gen wanted to meet us today, but she's away for the weekend with Wolfe."

"I'll take good care of you. Our outdoor runs are mostly full, since it's such a beautiful day, but there are still some inside. I just want to sit down with you in the adoption center so we can discuss a few things and I can make sure you're properly fit."

"Great."

Arilyn led her to a small room cheerfully decorated with animal posters, signs, chalkboards with scribbles galore, and a cute corner with a green rug, a small TV, and a comfy couch with a slipcover stenciled with dogs. A small desk with a few wooden chairs was placed on the far right. "This is our cuddle area when one of our volunteers feels like chilling with one of the animals and watching a movie."

"Hope it's not *Old Yeller*."

Arilyn laughed. "Happy movies only. We have DVDs of *Beethoven*, *K-9*, *Lady and the Tramp*, and *Benji*. That should cover all tastes. Take a seat here, and I'll ask a few questions.

Oh, do you mind if we have someone else join us? He's ready to adopt and I've decided to take care of you both."

"Of course; the more the merrier."

"Am I late?"

Izzy stiffened.

No. No, no, no, no, no . . .

She looked up. Slowly. And there he was, standing over her. All tall and dreamy-like, straight from a Hollywood set. Burnished hair, hip cocked, worn jeans cupping his ass and legs like they worshipped him. A navy-blue plaid button-down shirt was casually open at the neck, with the sleeves rolled up, showing off corded forearms and hands that could make a woman weep. Work boots clad his feet. Had he been doing work in his house? The image of him on a ladder with a hammer made her tummy tumble.

Arilyn gave him a hug, clueless about Izzy's sudden gripping tension. "Good to see you, Devine. About time you decided to adopt. I've been working on you awhile."

He grinned, those white teeth flashing. "Like you said, it's a big decision and I didn't want to make it lightly."

"I agree. Izzy's on the same path, so I thought it would be fun to do this together."

Izzy closed her eyes momentarily.

So. Much. Fun.

Liam shot her a knowing grin. She wanted to kiss it off his handsome face. "Good to see you again, Isabella. How've you been?"

Oh, he was bad. His wicked gaze probed all her delicate girly parts and sprung them to life. She looked like a mess, too. Crazy hair 'cause she hadn't tried to tame it, with old jeans, sneakers, and a Mets jersey. "Just ducky," she drawled.

His grin was pure delight. "Mets, huh? I'm a Yanks fan myself."

Alexa would say it was fate they weren't meant to be together. Her sister was more of a fanatic than she was, but Izzy had learned early on to appreciate baseball and to root for the Mets at all costs. It had been a huge issue with Alexa's husband, Nick, but eventually, her family had come around. Could she bring another Yanks fan to her family table?

Never.

"Figures. Just another confirmation of our differences," she muttered.

"You're saying baseball is a deal breaker in your relationships?" he asked curiously.

"Absolutely."

Arilyn looked interested in the exchange. "Over baseball? That's crazy."

"You don't know my family."

Liam rocked back on his heels. "I'm flexible. I can change teams."

She stared at him with pure indignation. "That's an insult to your team," she pointed out. "New York fans don't just change teams easily. It's completely disrespectful!"

Instead of fighting back or getting offended, he considered her outrage with a reasonableness that made her want to lose her temper. "Let's just say if I had to choose between the woman I wanted and the Yanks, I could live without baseball." His eyes dazzled pale-blue sparks, stealing her breath. "Not her."

She froze in place. The world dropped away as they stared at one another.

"That's romantic, Devine," Arilyn said in her musical voice.

Izzy managed to blow out an annoyed breath. "It's still screwed-up. Some things should never be asked for. Even in love."

"Let me ask you this, Isabella. If you fell in love with a Yanks fan, would you force him to choose between you and his team?"

Damn him. She wriggled with discomfort, hating the question. "Are we going to see the dogs?"

Arilyn glanced between them with fascination. "Sure, but I want to hear your answer, too."

Liam lifted a brow and waited.

"No, I wouldn't. It would just be . . . wrong."

"Exactly. Thank you for proving my point."

His words held that faint warning again, though it was wrapped up in pure sex appeal and masculine demand. Got her hot every time. Why did he have to be so droolworthy? It was completely unfair.

Arilyn broke the stare standoff and sat behind the desk. "Let's just do a quick intake now that you're both here, and go see the dogs." Devine took a seat next to her, his long length barely fitting in the small wooden chair. His hard thigh brushed hers. Goose bumps peppered her skin. "First off, is there any particular breed or mix you're interested in? Any breed you're concerned about?"

Izzy shook her head. "I love all breeds and am open to any of them."

"I agree," Liam said.

"Great. How about any restrictions to your home or property? Other animals? Limited time?"

"Since I have a great boss, I'm sure I'll be able to run home and let my dog out," Izzy said with a grin. Arilyn grinned back. "And as we both know, the bungalow is perfect."

Liam scratched his head. "My house is set up already with a fenced-in yard and plenty of room. My work schedule could sometimes be a problem if I hold down double shifts, but I may be able to get my neighbor to check in. Or I can trade off some shifts if I need some extra time home in the beginning."

Arilyn nodded. "Great, I think that's reasonable." She went through a quick checklist, making sure they knew all the responsibilities of pet ownership. "Now, is there a certain age bracket you prefer?"

"No puppies," they both blurted out in unison.

Izzy looked at him. "You, too?" she asked.

"I just spent endless months renovating. I'm not up for a puppy."

They smiled at each other in understanding.

"Got it," Arilyn said. "Too bad—we have the most adorable litter ready to be adopted. They'll probably be all gone by tomorrow. Let's head out and start meeting the animals."

Izzy trailed behind her, noting Liam matched her pace to hang back. "How's work?" he asked.

His casual question set the tone. Distance. She needed to cultivate friendly distance. "Good. I'm learning to program the matchups and spreadsheets, and it's fascinating work. I never thought science could merge into the art of matching up two people for a relationship, but Kinnections proved me wrong."

"I didn't know you liked computers."

"Yeah; I have a tiny piece of nerdism within me. Something about all that useless data turning into something that can run an empire inspires me. I'm good at data matching and finding the holes in code."

"I'm not surprised. It holds just enough challenge to keep you interested."

"Exactly." He tugged at her hair in a playful gesture that made her smile. The damning words tumbled from her lips too fast to stop. "I'm assuming you're working with Kate now to find your match?"

He looked pleased at her question. Too pleased. "Why? Interested in who they come up with for me?"

Her foot stumbled over a rock, and he reached out and grabbed her arm, steadying her. A flash of heat tingled her nerve endings. "No. Yes. I mean, no, no—of course not. That's your personal business now."

"So you haven't thought about me or that kiss?"

"No. It was a way for us to reach closure. I've put it behind us, and so should you."

His deep laugh mixed with the sharp tones of barking. She narrowed her gaze. "What's so funny?" she hissed.

"You. I finally got you to lie."

"Here we go," Arilyn chirped merrily. She opened the gate where cages spread out over the green grass. For the next two hours, she led them to each dog, describing the personality, habits, common behaviors, and history. Izzy met small dogs, big dogs, white dogs, mottled dogs, shy and nosy ones, the calm and the playful. Breeds were a potpourri of color and beauty, and she enjoyed each visit, treasuring the time and saying a quick prayer for each one to find his or her forever home as she went from one dog to the next.

Liam walked two of them, and Izzy walked three. Finally, Arilyn led them inside the house, greeting the various volunteers along the way. "There are ten more dogs inside, plus the new litter. I think Rocky may be a great fit for you, Devine. He's a boxer with a great personality."

"Sounds good."

Sharp barks and activity surrounded them. The smell of dogs and antiseptic drifted in the air. "We have them in the playroom right now so you can have fun meeting half of them at a time. We try to get them out of their cages as much as possible, so many of our volunteers take time just to sit in the playroom for an hour or two and give them attention."

Arilyn reached out to unlock the door when a man with buzz-cut brown hair and frantic eyes rushed up. "Arilyn, we have a huge problem with Hugo—can you come over for a minute?"

"Sure. Excuse me, guys. Can you hang out here for me?"

"Absolutely, go," Izzy said. Arilyn ran off and Izzy shook her head, amazed at her friend's knowledge and her dedication to the animals.

"So, what do you think?" Liam asked, leaning against the wall. "Feel kismet with any of the dogs so far?"

Izzy sighed. "I adore many of them and see them as a possibility. The white terrier, Cynthia, was a nice fit. But I don't feel that crazy connection like I thought I would. Is that stupid? Maybe that's just a fairy tale and it doesn't exist anyway. I don't want to not take a dog because I have an idea in my mind something is real when it isn't."

He reached out and ran a finger down her cheek. She released her breath in a long rush, mirroring a longing sigh. "I believe it. And that's the same problem with me today. I haven't felt that need to own a particular dog yet. One who speaks to me and demands I take him or her home. One with a soul connection."

"Maybe we're both just dreamers who'll get hurt," she whispered.

"Maybe not."

Within the chaos, there was a perfect circle of silence around them. He lowered his head, and Izzy knew he was about to kiss her again. She also knew she couldn't stop him.

Didn't want to stop him.

"There you two are!" A pretty blonde with a high pony-tail and dazzling smile jumped in front of them, breaking the moment. She wore a hot-pink T-shirt with the slogan KEEP CALM AND RESCUE ON. "Come with me to see them. We have to be quick because they're in high demand."

"Umm, I don't think we're the people you're looking for."

The blonde wasn't listening, pushing them down the hall like they were a couple of disobedient puppies. "Come, come; time is wasting. I have two picked out for you I thought you'd like to meet first. One is the runt, and she gets a bit nervous at times, so just be careful."

Liam tried to speak up. "No, see, we're with Arilyn and waiting for her to get back."

"Oh, we adore Arilyn around here, but she's very busy, and we did talk to each other over the phone."

"Actually, we didn't and—"

"Here we are. Let me just grab them for you."

Izzy looked down and lost her voice.

Puppies.

There were about half a dozen of them, with large, floppy ears and short, stout legs and the biggest, brownest eyes she'd ever seen. Their coats varied, but they were mostly a mix of gorgeous colors, like a canvas where a toddler decided to throw paint. White and black and reddish brown and gray, all mingled and mottled over their bodies. They rolled over one another in endless play, making little barks and mewling. Three of them were cuddled up in a heap, snoring. One was trying desperately to topple the water dispenser, jumping up and growling at the metal as if it were an enemy.

The blonde scooped up two and plopped one in Izzy's arms. She pointed to the puppy. "That's the runt of the litter. She's a bit shy, but she has spirit." She turned to Liam and pushed the second puppy into his embrace. "You have the boy. For some reason, these two have been very close. They're bonded in some way. Always together. We'd prefer to keep them in the same household, if possible."

Izzy looked down into the most adorable face she'd ever seen in her life. The puppy was reddish-brown with white splotches, and had Dumbo-like ears that practically covered her cheeks. Nose twitching, tiny puppy teeth nibbled at her finger as she stroked the velvety snout, and a warm tongue lashed out to lick her. The smell of brand-new life and deliciousness swarmed her senses. With a little whimper, the puppy wriggled for a better position, and her silky fur was a caress against Izzy's bare skin, offering warm comfort. She kissed her face, enjoying her puppy breath, laughing at the fur ball in her grasp with the big brown eyes and too-large feet and lapping tongue.

And then, just like that, Izzy fell in love.

She looked over at Liam. He looked just as entranced with the wriggling body in his arms. A softness in his face fascinated her, and she caught a hint of how he'd look with his child in his arms, as if humbled by the opportunity to be able to love someone that much.

Her heart crumbled. She was a goner.

Ponytail Lady kept talking. "They're a mix of beagle and basset hound, so they may have a bit of a howl. They should reach an average weight of fifty pounds, no more, the runt definitely less so. Fully tested and weaned. What do you think?"

Liam lifted his gaze and met hers.

Perfect understanding passed between them.

"We'll take them," they said together.

"What are you doing?"

Arilyn marched up to them, a look of horror flickering over her face. "Deb, why are you showing them the puppies? I told them to wait for me; they're only interested in the older dogs."

Deb looked back and forth between them in pure confusion. "Wait—I thought this was the couple I had an appointment with. We didn't speak on the phone?"

"We tried to tell you," Liam pointed out.

"I'm sorry, Arilyn, my mistake. Here, let me take them back." Deb reached for the puppy Izzy held, but Izzy backed away, protecting the little runt in her arms.

"No! She's mine. I want her."

Arilyn's mouth dropped open. For the first time in her life, Izzy realized her friend actually owned a temper. "Absolutely not. You are not ready to cope with the stress of owning a puppy. I'll set you up with a dog who's potty trained already, and you'll have the structure you're both looking for. Devine, you agree, right?"

Liam shook his head. Within his strong arms, his puppy looked small but well protected. "No. I want him. He's mine."

Deb backed away from the mess. "Umm, I gotta go, Arilyn. They need help in the cat room. See ya!"

Her ponytail bobbed as she took off.

Izzy raised her chin, ready to fight for her puppy. No one was going to separate them. Liam inched toward her to unite in the stand against Arilyn.

"Guys, this is crazy! This is why I try to keep people away from the puppies." She closed her eyes and moaned. "Listen to me—you need to be reasonable. They will wreck your house and poop everywhere and cry. They're like newborns and the first few weeks are critical. Plus, these two are super close. Do you really want to separate them?"

Emotion washed over her. Izzy's lower lip trembled. No.

She couldn't give her up now, just when they'd found each other.

Liam cleared his throat. "Listen, they can meet at the dog park. Isabella and I both live in Verily. They can play with Robert and Pinky, and we can structure playdates together. It can work."

Ignoring the knowledge this would tie her to Liam, she jumped in with desperation. "Yes! That would work, right?"

Arilyn nibbled at her lower lip. "Maybe. Yes, that could definitely work. It would be extremely difficult to find them a home together anyway, so this would be the next best thing." Turning into the fierce warrior she was, she pointed her finger at both of them. "Are you truly ready for this? It really does resemble being a parent to a newborn. You both need to feel one hundred percent committed to training and providing structure."

In response, the runt suddenly made a choking noise. Izzy quickly held her up higher to see what the problem was.

And then her puppy threw up.

Sad, mortified eyes stared into hers. Izzy realized this would be her new life, and it might not be easy. Vomit stuck to her clothes and was splattered on her pants. She looked at Arilyn.

"See what I mean? This one's nervous and when she gets stressed, she throws up!"

Ridiculous tears burned Izzy's eyes. "I don't care. I love her," she burst out.

"I love him, too," Liam said stubbornly. "We're taking them."

Arilyn stared at both of them hard, then slowly began to grin. The grin grew by epic proportions, turning into a belly laugh that exploded in the room. Both puppies stopped wriggling and turned to look at her. "Yes. You two are official goners. You found your canine mates. Let's go get you set up so you can take them home."

Izzy cuddled her puppy and happily followed her friend out.

eight

"NO, HAN SOLO. Don't chew. You'll get sick."

Exhausted, he reached down to pluck Han from chewing the last good leg of his coffee table. He settled the pup on his chest, hoping he'd relax for an hour. A minute. Hell, a second would work at this point.

Instead, he caught the scrunched-up face Han got when he needed to pee.

"No! No, let's go out, let's go out," he sang crazily, scrambling up from the couch to grab the leash. "Hold it, Han, hold it—no!"

Too late. Pee scattered on the carpet and over his hand.

"Yuck! Ugh, that's disgusting." Devine shot into the kitchen, grabbed a mass of paper towels, and swiped the pup's belly. It must've tickled, because Han began to squirm and desperately lick, resembling the cutest miniature Ewok he'd ever seen.

He melted. "Aww, okay, you tried, buddy. Right? Let me clean this up." As he cleaned up the carpet, he decided to pull it up next weekend and go back to wood floors. Sure, they were a bit scratched, but it would work while Han was young, and then he'd put in the investment to strip them and make them new again. After the peeing was done.

Devine scrubbed and wondered what time it was. He'd been in a constant time warp of discipline, getting Han to walk on the leash, and trying to be on top of accidents. When had he eaten? Ah hell, forget it. It was early, but he'd try to get to bed and catch up on sleep. Weren't puppies supposed to sleep for most of the day, or was that some kind of cruel lie to woo owners?

Han didn't like sleep. He liked trouble.

After Devine cleaned up, he took Han for his final walk, then got him ready with his crate. Arilyn had explained it was important for puppies to sleep in a crate at night for structure and to limit damage. Later on, you could bring them to your bed, but if you started off wrong, you were stuck with bad habits forever.

Devine didn't believe in bad habits. Sure, last night was a nightmare with no sleep, but tonight he was sure they'd both pass out cold.

"Come on, Han, time for bed."

The pup anticipated the move and took off, running furiously around the house and leading Devine on a crazy chase. How could the little bugger be so hard to catch? Finally, he dove and got him, scooping him up and settling him inside his crate. He'd made it warm and cozy, with stuffed toys, approved chewy bones, one of his shirts for his scent, and a blanket. Still, Han didn't agree with him on the home design, because he went frantic, crying and scratching at his crate in an effort to get to Devine.

"No, I'm sorry, Han. You sleep in the crate. I sleep in the bedroom."

The hound howl was long and painful. Devine rubbed his head. What should he do? The poor thing looked so miserable. But then he remembered when Stone began taking Pinky to work because she'd totally manipulated him with her crying. No, he was stronger. More disciplined. He'd do what Arilyn and the *Raising a Puppy* book said.

Exhibiting confidence he didn't feel, he turned out the lights and headed into his bedroom. Usually his oasis, he'd decorated it with forest greens and earth colors. His furniture was a gorgeous dark wood, and the bed had a leather-padded headboard. The decorations were sparse, but each had meaning. The framed picture of his family at his brother's wedding. The antique tapestry chair he'd found at a garage sale and restored on his own as a side project. The painting of Tuscany's rolling hills drenched in light, where he'd always wanted to go on his honeymoon. His framed diplomas from college and the police academy. A safe haven to sleep, with no outside stress.

He pulled on an old T-shirt and sweat shorts and climbed into bed.

Then listened to an hour of nonstop howling and crying.

Devine tried with every iota of his being to ignore Han and sleep. But the howls shredded every nerve ending until he was a jumping, shaking mess. Finally, he marched out of the bedroom and knelt beside the crate, where Han made a frantic effort to escape his prison.

The book said hold a hard line. Arilyn had warned him of what could happen. What was he going to do?

He reached for the phone and punched in her number.

"Hello?"

"You gotta help me, Isabella."

"Liam? What's the matter? Is your puppy okay?"

He held the phone up to Han's wild cries. "Does that sound like he's okay?"

Her voice was husky with exhaustion. "You put him in the crate, right? Did he sleep at all last night?"

"No; neither of us did. I'm going out of my head. I took off an extra day so I can make some headway with his training, but I haven't slept, and he cries if I'm not with him, and he pees everywhere, and I'm so fucking tired. How are you coping?"

Her sigh told him everything. "I'm not. Same story here. Leia won't sleep and she tears through the house, and I already lost a shoe 'cause she's so small she wriggled into the tiny crack in my closet and had a leather feast."

"Yeah, I lost three table legs. You named her Leia?"

"Isn't that sweet? Princess Leia, to be exact. What did you name yours?"

He paused. Somehow he had a feeling she wouldn't like it. "Umm, Han. Han Solo."

Silence.

He rubbed his head and Han shrieked in frustration that he was still stuck in his crate. The voice on the line shook with temper. "What? You named him Han Solo? That's ridiculous! People are going to think we came up with that as a couple! Why did you have to do that?"

He growled back. "You don't have the rights to *Star Wars*—I always wanted a pet named after Han. He's my favorite character!"

"Yeah, but Leia is mine and I thought of it first."

"I had my name picked out for years."

"So did I! We're going to look idiotic at the dog park! Why couldn't you be more original?"

"Why couldn't *you*?" he practically shouted. "Listen, I don't have time for this stupid argument right now. You gotta come over."

"I'm not coming over!"

"I'm serious, Isabella. I need help. I'm on the edge. Arilyn said not to let him in the bed, and last night I ended up trying to sleep on the rug next to him but he cried all night. I'm falling apart. Bring over Leia. Maybe they miss each other."

A groan came over the line. "Maybe you should call Arilyn. I'm in my pajamas. I'm tired."

"Is Leia letting you sleep?"

A pause. "No. It's bad here. Very bad."

"Then I'll come to you. I'll be right over."

"No! Dammit, okay, I'll come over there. What's your address?"

He gave it to her. "Hurry."

"Look, I'm not interested in any shenanigans. I'm coming solely to help the dogs, so you have to promise not to make any moves."

"Are you kidding me? I have no interest in shenanigans either. Yes, you're hot and I want you bad, but I'm tired and cranky, and I just want to make him stop howling and peeing and chewing. Got it?"

"Fine."

The phone clicked.

Devine faced Han. Puppy teeth bit at the crate's bars, and he let out fierce howls, shaking his large ears when they flopped in his face. "Fine. We're getting company, so you can stay up later tonight." He clicked open the door and scooped the puppy out. Raising him up to his direct vision, he spoke firmly. "There will be no more of this nonsense. When I declare bedtime, you need to sleep. But Isabella and Leia are coming over, so you get a respite."

Han licked the tip of his nose and sighed with canine satisfaction.

And damned if Devine's heart didn't melt like the pussy he was.

"I CANNOT BELIEVE I'm doing this," Izzy muttered under her breath, pulling into the circular driveway. She squinted through the dark to make out the outline of a decent-size ranch with a fenced-in yard and a small covered porch. Her curiosity was piqued. She'd finally get to see his house.

Little whimpers poured from the backseat. "I know, sweetie; we're here. You're going to see your brother." She got out of the car and slid the crate out, walking up the winding path. When he called, she'd been in a state of near tears from Leia's constant howling for the second night in a row. His crazy request to come over actually sounded sane. At this point, she'd try anything, even though she was still mad he had ruined her unique name by stealing another character for his own puppy. So unfair.

The door opened before she could knock. Her heart pounded and her body went on instant alert. How was this fair? He was literally a mess. Hair sticking up, a rough five o'clock shadow hugging his jaw, wearing a faded T-shirt and black sweat shorts, and sporting bare feet. She'd barely been able to pull on some old jeans, a blue sweatshirt with a hole in it, and flip-flops. Her hair was pulled up in a pony-tail and her makeup was almost nonexistent. She looked awful.

Yet he looked more delectable than ever. She wanted to pounce, climb on him, lick at that stubble, tear off his clothes, and ride him hard.

The image slammed into her brain, and she shook her head hard to dissipate it.

"Thank God you came. Come in." He took the crate

from her and set it on the earth-tone carpet, then shut the door. "Han, I have a surprise for you," he called out.

A whizzing ball of fur flew to her and attacked her ankles, nibbling on the strap of her shoe and wildly licking her toes. She burst into giggles and picked him up, placing a kiss on his snout. "That tickles, you little fur ball," she crooned. "Have you been torturing Liam?"

"Prisoners of war should be locked up with a puppy to take care of. That would teach 'em," he muttered, pulling Leia into his arms. "Come here, sweetheart. You have your brother to play with now."

A shiver raced down her spine at his low, crooning voice. Her nipples twisted into hard points, and her panties dampened. Crap. He had to stop talking like that to her puppy or she'd break.

They placed the puppies on the floor and watched them hurl themselves together in a crazy embrace. Tumbling around and around, nipping at ears, legs entangled, it seemed like a joyous homecoming that got Izzy all mushy.

"Have you slept at all this weekend?" he asked.

"An hour or two at the most," she admitted.

"How bad are the accidents?"

Izzy sighed. "I'm glad I don't have wall-to-wall carpets. At least I can pull up the throw rugs temporarily."

"Yeah, but do you take her outside on the leash forever, and then when she comes back in, she pees right in front of you like she thinks you're an idiot?"

Izzy laughed. "Yep. They're not in control of their bladders, I think. Arilyn said if we keep taking them out, eventually they'll get it."

"Let's just hope it's not a year from now. I thought I was a strong person. But I'm cracking, Isabella, and it's only been a weekend."

"I know. We need to dig deep and things will get better. They're babies."

"Yeah, you're right. I love the little bugger, too. Can I get you a Coke? Tea?"

"Water would be great for now."

Letting the puppies wrestle freely, he headed to the open kitchen overlooking the spacious living room. Izzy walked around, taking in the layout. It was a beautiful house. Dark wood furnishings and neutral colors screamed masculinity, from the leather sectional to the large espresso dining table. A surplus of technological equipment such as a megascreen television, speakers, and shelves full of DVDs and books was scattered about. The ceilings held a crisscross of beams, adding a bit of the rustic. A fireplace framed in distressed brick took up the far wall, surrounded by crooked shelves holding an array of books. An antique-looking cabinet painted red was the only shock of color besides a few green, leafy plants strategically placed around the room. The walls were mostly bare except for a family photo here and there. No throw pillows or blankets or feminine touches softened the stark look. The kitchen had a butcher-block counter, updated stainless-steel appliances, and nice ceramic floor tiles. The table held a MacBook Air, several folders, and the daily clutter that marked a well-lived-in house.

"Your place is nice," she called out. "Did you say you renovated it?"

He walked over and handed her a glass of water with lemon. "Yeah; I bought it for a clearance sticker price. It was run-down and abandoned, so the bank sold it to me. I redid the front porch, gutted the kitchen, and built a deck on the back."

"Yourself?"

He grinned. "Some of it. The other stuff I hired contractors for, but I learned a lot. I like to fiddle with stuff around the house. It's soothing."

Izzy imagined him stripped down, hammering at a wall, tool belt hanging low around his waist to show off his impressive abs, and felt a bit woozy. She avoided his gaze, knowing his police skills were too sharp. If he scented weakness, he might try to take advantage.

Her inner voice laughed with mocking hilarity. Yeah, right. She'd end up being the one to take advantage of him. When it came to Liam, she reacted like a sex-starved, love-struck teen at a simple touch. Why did it feel so good? Like she was alive again after existing in a black-and-white world?

"Sit. Let them play. Forgive me if I start snoring in the middle of a sentence."

She relaxed. The man was in no shape to take advantage. She set her drink on the coffee table, tucked her leg underneath her, and leaned against the cool leather. He sat next to her, leaving a comfortable few inches between them. Still, his body threw off delicious waves of masculine heat. "You going to work tomorrow?" he asked.

"No. I took one extra day so I could get Leia settled in. You?"

"Same thing. I had the weekend free and got McCoy to take over my shift tomorrow. Think I can train Han in one more day?"

"No. We're screwed."

He sighed. "Yeah. At least I'm not on nights for a while, and I already lined up my neighbor's daughter to come take care of him in the early afternoon."

"I'm lucky, too. Arilyn's grandfather said he could help during the week if I'm working late, and I can go home on my lunch hour to take care of her."

"Patrick is a good guy. We hang out at Ray's Billiards together. He's a trip. Can hold his damn whiskey better than any of the guys at the station."

Izzy saw the moment he stiffened, as if realizing how easy it was to talk about getting drunk. "You know I don't care, right, Liam? Drinking is a way of socializing. If I hadn't overindulged on a consistent basis, I could enjoy a drink or two, too."

He tilted his head, studying her face. "Are you also an alcoholic?"

"It wasn't as much the alcohol as the drugs, but I decided to cut that out of my life also. One tempts the other. My father is an alcoholic, and since it's been documented that genes could have an effect, I don't need to tempt fate any more than I did."

"Smart."

She liked the way he took her answers and understood. He asked when he was curious, not afraid to be real.

A crash to the floor made her jump.

She craned her neck around as Liam cursed softly and headed to inspect the damage. "Okay, you little monsters, it's a good thing that didn't break." He picked up the metal picture frame from the side table. Scooping up Leia and Han, he walked to the center of the room where they could be carefully watched. "Play over here and—ah shit!"

Izzy winced and watched as Leia made a familiar noise and retched all over his shirt.

Slapping a hand firmly over her mouth, she held back the giggles ready to explode from the look on Liam's face. Disgust, horror, and shock combined as he stared mutely down at the puppy, who now looked like she felt much better and was giving him the famous look all females did when they were in trouble.

Brown puppy eyes wide with apology, she whimpered and nudged his hand, licking gently.

"I assume she was nervous?" he asked steadily.

She tried to keep a straight face. "Yep. Arilyn said the

vet checked her out thoroughly and declared it a nervous habit she'll grow out of."

"Fantastic." He plopped them down, wrinkling his nose. "Ugh, I smell." Pulling the fabric away from his body, he peeled off his shirt. "Let me throw this in the wash; be right back."

She refused to watch his naked retreating back, so she sipped her water and watched the siblings play. She heard the faucet run and then quiet footsteps returning. "I'm making you pick her up next time until she grows out of it."

"Sorry, I figured she . . ." Izzy trailed off, words deserting her.

He hadn't put on another shirt.

As he stood in front of her, chest bare, she shook with a desperate need to close the distance and touch him. Whorls of golden hair lay scattered over a muscled chest, tightly defined. His abs looked rock-hard. Her fingers curled into tight fists, craving to trace the line of hair down the middle that disappeared under the waistband of his shorts. He looked like a Greek god, feet braced, hands on hips, not aware that his masculine beauty and strength would cause any woman's heart to stop, stutter, and restart.

He caught her reaction and stilled. The air between them became charged. Burning heat shot from his aqua-blue eyes and he caught his breath, as if trying to make a decision. She stared at him, helpless to move.

"Keep looking at me that way, and we're going to have a problem," he warned softly.

Izzy jumped, tearing her gaze away with painful effort. She cleared her throat. "Sorry."

"I'm not." He sat down beside her but kept the space between them. "I just don't want to feel punch-drunk from lack of sleep when I finally get you in my bed."

The declaration was easy and confident. She jerked her head back around and glared. "That's not gonna happen even when you're well rested, buddy."

A slow smile curved his lips. "Why do you think we both ended up in Verily?"

She thought about it, then shrugged. "Coincidence."

"No such thing. Didn't they talk in rehab about life's paths having meaning and meeting certain people in your life when it was meant to be?"

Uneasy, she shifted her weight. She was tempted to close down the whole conversation, but something urged her forward. "Actually, they did. We were taught to see purpose for our choices and to believe we are at this exact moment because it's in the bigger plan. How did you know?"

"I studied a lot about drug use in the academy. I felt if I knew as much about the people using, and their struggles to get clean, it would help me be a better cop. I've gone to Narcotics Anonymous meetings."

Of course he had. Because that was the type of man he was. Emotion washed over her. He was so . . . good. Every action was done with the purpose of being better, digging deeper, giving more. "I'm not surprised," she said quietly. "You, Liam Devine, are an extraordinary man."

Shock filled his beautiful blue eyes. "I wish you could see as clearly as I do, Isabella. You're just as extraordinary. And I believe we met again in Verily because our story wasn't over yet. I believe it's just beginning."

The breath left her body. How could she fight this man? His words and his actions and his physical presence pulled her down like an undertow, trying to overwhelm her. And as she fought to swim, struggling to pry herself away from this extreme connection, Izzy began to wonder why she was trying to fight so hard in the first place.

Silence fell over the room.

Suddenly, she realized silence wasn't a good thing when there were two puppies in the same room. She jerked upward. "Oh no, Liam; it's quiet. Where are they?"

He flew off the couch, frantically looking around, then stopped. A grin curved his lips. "You gotta see this."

She rose and looked over. The puppies were inside Han's crate, heads together, paws entwined, snuggled within the blanket. Low snores came from the cage. "They're exhausted," she said with amusement. "I think that's one of the cutest things I've ever seen."

"Agreed. Now let's see if *we* can finally get some sleep." He quietly closed the crate door and latched it, then turned. "Take my bed; I'll take the couch."

"No, I'm fine with the couch. A few hours are all I need."

"Absolutely not."

"Umm, to be honest, I don't drop into sleep easily, even when I'm tired. I need to relax with TV first."

"I have the perfect thing for both of us." He headed to the television, slid in a DVD, and started it. He walked to the closet and returned moments later with a large blanket and a small pillow. "Mind if I watch a bit with you?"

"Of course not."

He settled on the other side of the couch, propping his feet up on the leather ottoman. The blanket was big enough for two, so she rested her pillow on the arm of the sofa and stretched out under the warm, fuzzy material. As the credits for *The Empire Strikes Back* scrolled across the screen, a yawn split her lips.

"Do you hear that?" he whispered.

"What?"

"Quiet. Not a sound. I want to weep with joy."

She smiled, tucked the blanket under her chin, and began laughing.

"What's so funny?" he asked curiously.

"Your blanket. It's chartreuse."

He gave her a fierce frown. "That session was confidential. And I got that as a gift."

"Sure." He grabbed her feet and tickled her through the blanket, forcing small giggles to erupt. "Okay, I'm sorry!"

"Forgiven. This time." But he was grinning back at her, and Izzy wanted to touch his face, cup his jaw, trace the lush curve of his lips, press her forehead to his. A shudder of want swept through her, so she turned back to the movie and tried to remind herself it was all for the best.

Soon, she fell asleep.

nine

ZZY SURFACED OUT OF A DEEP SLEEP, fuzzy tendrils of drowsiness still clinging to keep her from being fully awake. Still dark. Rustling behind her. A low, husky voice whispering. She blinked, trying to remember, and then her surroundings clicked into her awareness.

"Liam?" she whispered, shifting on the couch.

"Shhh, go back to sleep." A latch locked into place. Movement came from her right, and then he was kneeling at her side. "It's only five a.m. I took the puppies out and they settled right back in."

"You walked them both?"

"Of course. You need your sleep." He reached out and stroked back the tangled hair that had escaped her ponytail. "Do you want me to carry you into my bed? I can sleep out here."

"No." Her hand lifted of its own accord to cup his cheek. She caressed his rough stubble, then traced the line of his jaw, over his lips. So soft. He pressed a kiss to her fingers.

"Sweetheart, you're half-asleep. Rest."

God, he felt so good. His breath held the scent of mint. Had he brushed his teeth this morning? Even in the shadows, his pale eyes glowed like the embers of a fire ready to flare up. No man had ever gazed at her with such intensity, such devotion. Why was she fighting so hard again? To give him away to another woman? Oh, but how her heart ached to have him to herself for just a little while, without worrying about the future. Without worrying she'd never be enough for him. Her other hand reached out to stroke his thick hair, like rough silk. A slight groan rumbled from his chest, now covered in a soft T-shirt. "You feel so good," she whispered. "I'm so tired of fighting this."

He stiffened. "I don't want you to fight it, Isabella. I just want to hold you. Bring you pleasure. But not when you don't know what you're doing."

Maybe it was the dark, and the loneliness that cut through her at the thought of him walking away. Maybe it was the culmination of every moment spent with him, or the slowly mounting hunger growing inside of her to be part of him again. Izzy had no idea—she only knew she wanted him so badly, her entire being shook with pure need.

She tilted her head up. Moved closer. Slowly, afraid to break the spell, she pressed her forehead to his, her hands stroking his rough cheeks, tracing the plump line of his lower lip. He shuddered against her.

"I know exactly what I'm doing," she murmured as her lips met his.

She kissed him, long and slow. He let her lead as she savored the taste of him, the heat of his mouth, the flavor of his tongue, the soft firmness of his lips. With a growl, he slanted his mouth to take the kiss deeper, pressing her back against the cushions, and climbed on top of her.

Every hard muscle cradled her curves. They feasted on each other as his hands explored her body, cupping her breasts, his lips breaking free from her mouth to nibble and suck on the length of her neck. Her hands gripped his shoulders, looking for an anchor, and his teeth bit delicately against her tattoo, causing her to cry out. He soothed with his tongue, murmuring her name, and then a fierce storm of need crashed through her, and Izzy became crazed to touch and taste every part of his body.

Ripping the blanket aside, he tugged off her clothes in seconds, whisking her out of her tiny panties until she lay naked underneath him. Tearing off his shirt, he threw it on the floor with the pile of clothes. Already damp and throbbing with arousal, she arched against him, his erection notched perfectly between her thighs. He rocked slowly, dragging against her clit, the soft cotton the only barrier between them. She panted and dug her fingernails into his hard shoulders, urging him to go faster.

But he ignored her, keeping the pace slow and steady as his head dipped to brush his lips against the hard tip of a nipple. With teasing strokes, he plucked and licked until her breasts were so sensitive, one flick to her clit would make her shatter.

As if he knew, he laughed low in his throat and continued his torture, sucking on her nipple while his fingers played her body like a maestro. Stroking the swell of her body, the curve of her hip, he shifted his weight, pinning her wide open while his fingers dipped into the crease between her legs, gathering the wetness and pressing against her dripping entrance, refusing to go any further.

She exploded into a rage of need. Sinking her teeth into his meaty bicep, she worked her arms free and shoved down his shorts, wrapping her hands around the hot, hard shaft to rub and stroke, sliding over the wet tip where his own arousal leaked.

He cursed and bit her nipple in punishment. Jerked against her hands even as he slid his fingers deep into her pussy, giving her only a taste of what she craved. "Witch. I waited too long for this, dammit. I refuse to come in your hands like a horny teen."

"I like you as a horny teen," she teased, gasping when he increased the pace of his fingers, brushing the edge of her needy clit. "It hurts, Liam. I need you so much it hurts."

"Fuck. You're so hot and wet. What do you do to me?"

"What you do to me."

"I need to see you come. I need to know this is all for me. Don't close your eyes."

His sexy demand wrested shudders from her body, and she twisted to get closer but he pinned her down with an easy strength, sliding downward, parting her swollen lips and dipping his head between her thighs.

"Liam!"

His lips and tongue worked magic on her dripping core. His fingers curled and pumped into her with the perfect amount of pressure, bringing her right to the edge of climax, then keeping her there, hanging an inch from the abyss. Her heels dug into the couch cushions. He flicked his tongue against her nub, then gave a long, slow lick down her slit, lengthening the tension until a knot formed in her belly and every muscle clenched against the rising orgasm threatening to crash over her.

"Oh, please," she wrung out, twisting her hips with desperation.

"Eyes on me, Isabella."

Forcing her lids to lift, she looked down at him, golden head bent over her, ravishing her body with a ferocious eroticism that racked her with convulsions. His lips opened and he sucked her clit hard, plunging his fingers deep into her pussy.

She came, exploding into tiny pieces as she crammed her hand in her mouth to muffle her screams. He kept up the pressure and she jerked with her release. He let her ride out a second tiny orgasm until she collapsed beneath him.

She heard him mutter something under his breath. She

watched him with a bone-deep satisfaction as he tore open a condom wrapper, shoved his shorts all the way down, and covered himself. Grasping her ankles, he pushed her legs higher and farther apart until her feet rested on his broad shoulders. Poised at her entrance, he sunk his cock inside her inch by slow inch, watching her face with a shattering intensity that ramped back up her arousal until she felt as if she'd never even had the first two orgasms. Finally, he stopped, breathing hard, buried inside her wet heat.

Sweat dripped from his brow. Their gazes locked, her body not only welcoming him but squeezing him hard, as if frantic to never let him go again. In that moment, her heart burst open, and a gorgeous light flowed into her veins, making tears sting her eyes.

"You've always been mine," he said.

Then he moved. Back and forth, ramming his hips to go stronger, deeper, plunging in and out with a ferocious rhythm that warned her he'd leave nothing of her behind—he'd strip down every wall and rip away every hiding spot, forcing her to surrender completely.

And she did. She gave it all back to him, with the sting of her nails and the bite of her teeth, with the ragged cries of his name and the thrust of her hips. And when they both exploded together, he wrapped his arms tight around her body, sheltering her from her very self, keeping her safe within the circle.

Racked by aftershocks of pleasure, she pressed her head to his shoulder and knew she would never, ever be the same person again.

He tugged the blanket over them, adjusted their position, and soon she was asleep again in his arms.

FOR THE FIRST TIME in his life, Devine was terrified.

He'd been scared before. In the academy, he'd worried he wouldn't be good enough for the force and would never achieve his dream of being a cop. On a drug bust, a guy had pulled a gun and shot at him, and in a flash he wondered if he was going to die. When his brother was in a car crash and his mother had called him to tell him the news, terror had struck deep as he worried if his brother would make it.

But he'd never fallen this hard for a woman and realized she might never be able to give him what he needed.

Now he knew. She was the one for him. The one he'd been waiting for to finally feel complete—just like in those damn chick flicks and romance novels.

Yes, Virginia, there is a Santa Claus.

There really was such a thing as soul mates and love at first sight. He'd proven it.

Stone would laugh his ass off if he had any idea.

Devine smothered a groan and made coffee while he waited for her to wake up. The puppies were happily playing with some old shoelaces and a bone after eating a crapload of dog food. But they both managed to actually pee outside and Devine almost did a happy dance right there on the public sidewalk. With a little sleep and that small accomplishment, he felt more hopeful he could wrangle this fatherhood thing.

Problem was, he'd do it best with Isabella by his side.

Everything was better with her. After last night, he confirmed the last question hovering in his mind. Had the connection he'd felt during sex been a beautiful dream, or could it be re-created?

The answer cracked him in the head like the barrel of a baseball bat.

No, it hadn't been a dream. Yes, it could be re-created. Yes, it was even better than the first time and gave him a glimpse of what their relationship could grow to become.

Would she give him a chance after this morning?

Or would she walk away again?

He poured himself a mug of coffee and headed toward the back deck. The puppies raced over to follow him, and he opened the sliding doors and stepped outside. The sharp cleanness of fall had closed in. Soon the leaves would turn, offering a blazing palette of golds and reds in the woods behind his house. It was one of his favorite seasons.

He leaned against the railing, took in the scenery, and sipped his coffee.

He could push. Stalk her. But how long could he keep up the pursuit if she was intent on sacrificing him to someone else? Was there a way to convince her she was everything he wanted?

He wished he could talk to someone. Crap—maybe he'd have to trust this awful vulnerability with Stone and hope to God he didn't torture him for the rest of their natural lives.

"Morning."

He turned at the husky voice. Wrapped up in the blanket, she held her own cup of coffee and came to stand beside him. A tentative smile curved her lips. In the streaming morning light, she took his breath away. A smattering of freckles dusted the bridge of her nose. Her bow lips were swollen from his kisses, and her gorgeous skin was unmarred by makeup. Crazy brown curls flew out in every direction. Her dark-blue eyes brimmed with the quiet satisfaction of a woman well loved.

He smiled slowly back. "Morning. I can make you tea. I know you don't like coffee."

"This is good. Sometimes I enjoy a cup here and there. Morning, Han; morning, Leia," she crooned as the pups raced over to give her kisses. She laughed, scratching their bellies, bestowing love, then straightened back up when they ran off to play.

They sipped the hot brew, relaxing into a comfortable silence. "I love the deck. I had no idea you had so much privacy here."

"Yeah, I usually grill and eat out here, and there are about five acres of woods behind that are protected so no one will be able to build. Another reason I bought the property. I hate neighbors on top of me."

"Yeah, it took me forever to warm up to Mrs. Blackfire, but Arilyn seems to have a great relationship with her now, so she rarely bothers me."

"Neighbor from hell?"

"Used to be. Guess everyone has a hidden soft side just ready to be tapped by the right person."

"Guess so."

He reached over and tugged her against him. Then stiffened. "You naked under that blanket?"

"Yep."

He paused. "On purpose?"

"Not really. I couldn't find my clothes."

"Ah shit, I'm sorry. I threw them in the laundry. They should be dry soon."

"Nice plan."

He laughed, stroking her hair. "Cops need to make their own luck sometimes."

"Ah, so you set up your targets, huh?"

"I think that came out wrong." He stared at her for a while. "Isabella?"

"Yeah?"

"I'd really like you to drop that blanket."

He held his breath, knowing he'd pushed. Stupid. He should've been cool and let her lead. Maybe she wanted to talk about what this morning meant. He should've suppressed some of his hunger for her, but it had only grown like a primitive beast looking to devour. He opened his mouth to apologize or something, and then—

She dropped the blanket.

He sucked in his breath. In the light, her body stunned his vision with ripe curves and cherry nipples and a neatly trimmed nest of dark-brown hair in the junction of her thighs. Her gorgeous skin reminded him of a succulent fruit, plump for picking and tasting. The tat scrolled over the top of her right breast only emphasized her earthiness and sensuality. His gaze feasted on every inch, and she allowed him to drink his fill.

"All you had to do was ask, Liam," she said seductively.

His dick was painfully hard, and he barely managed to tug her against him, tip her head back, and kiss her.

Lifting her naked body up into his arms, he stumbled inside, his hands grasping her glorious ass until he got to the middle of the living room and gave up on taking another step, caught in a crazed hunger to mark her right now, right here.

Dropping her to the carpet, insane with need, he ripped down his shorts and fumbled with a condom. He smelled the musky scent of her arousal, saw the wetness on her thighs, and turned wild. Flipping her over until she knelt on all fours in front of him, he cupped the globes of her ass, leaning over to bite and lick, wresting throaty moans and cries from her lips, then plunged into her heat.

He let out a roar as she squeezed him tight. Her wet heat urged him on, and he palmed her breasts, playing with her tight nipples while he fucked her, loved her, claimed her.

His name exploded in the air as she came, and he kept thrusting, savoring every ripple in her body as she shook within his grasp. Finally, his hips rammed home, and he let himself go, throwing his head back as he roared with satisfaction, letting the shocks of pleasure wash over him until he was emptied.

He slumped over her, pressing a kiss to her damp neck. She turned over to face him, her fingers touching his cheek. "Not too rough?" he asked.

"No," she said softly. "It was . . . everything."

He waited for more, but she just lay beside him, seemingly content.

"Do you . . . want to talk about anything?"

She shook her head.

And that's when he realized she wasn't going to talk about it.

Somehow she'd pushed all her doubts aside and was grabbing the moment. The problem was Devine didn't know how long his Camelot was going to last. But if he pushed the issue, demanded they talk about their relationship, she might flee. Maybe the best thing would be to follow her lead. No need to decide on terms or how they were together.

"Will you spend the day with me today?" he asked.

"Yeah, I'd like that. Maybe we can go to the dog—oh!"

She yelped and pulled back, and Han and Leia jumped on their naked bodies with pure joy, barking and licking, with scrambling paws and tangled limbs.

Devine protected his most precious part and Han walked on his back, furiously licking at his ear, causing him to burst into laughter.

Yeah, things were just about perfect. No reason to complicate things.

Communication was always overrated anyway.

ten

"IZZY, I HAVE GOOD NEWS."

She spun around in her chair to face Kate. "What's up?"

Kate crossed her arms, studying her face. "You look good, babe. Is there something going on?"

She grinned. The last month had been perfect. Leia was finally learning to pee outside and sleep in her crate without crying all night. She'd finished the project Arilyn had given her and had done so well, they now wanted her to help out more with the clients. She was going through a brief training program so she could help them with intake sessions.

Then there was Liam.

The thought of him made her insides mushy. Since that morning on his couch, they'd been together almost every day. They took the dogs to the park together, cooked dinner, watched *Star Wars*, and had crazy, wild, dirty, delicious sex.

All the time.

Her body was loose, and her spirit was light. For the first

time, she'd dumped all her worries and expectations and completely channeled her sister's favorite romance heroine: Scarlett O'Hara.

She would think about everything tomorrow.

When tomorrow came, Izzy pushed it off to the next day.

One glorious month later, she was still happily deflecting. How could she fight such a fierce connection? Liam was a powerful force and she didn't want to run any longer. She did what they had first taught her in rehab.

Take it one moment at a time. One day at a time.

Let your sense of control go and give it up to a higher power.

Believe you will be guided to the right path and have faith.

Every day, they grew closer, but Liam also refused to ask questions. They slipped naturally into a routine that was comfortable and never discussed the future. They also hadn't told anyone what was going on, so there was no feedback or good-natured advice that demanded analysis or thinking. Stone still didn't know, and Izzy kept her private life locked up from her friends and her sister.

For now.

She refocused on Kate. "Thanks. Leia is finally sleeping through the night, so I'm more energetic."

"Oh, that's wonderful! I know puppies are quite demanding, but things will only get better."

"Yeah, other than Leia eating half of my wicker basket and crapping out wicker pieces on my front yard. I got so nervous I took her to the vet."

Kate laughed. "Better than a pair of Louboutins."

Izzy gasped. "No! Robert?"

"No, I got Robert when he was older and past all those bad habits. Even worse. Arilyn bribed Kennedy to watch two foster puppies for a few hours one afternoon, and when she got back, Ken was holding the shredded shoes in one hand and the culprits in the other. Needless to say, she refused to ever dog-sit again."

Izzy shook her head. Kennedy's shoes were legendary. Now she didn't feel so bad about her wicker. "What did you want to talk about?"

"Oh, sorry. I swear my brain has been all fogged up lately, especially since that stupid stomach virus. I can't seem to remember anything. It's about Devine."

Izzy tried to look cool. "What about him?"

"I found his match!"

It took a few seconds for her to process Kate's announcement. She'd forgotten that Kinnections had been working to match Liam this entire time. Sickness crashed over her but she struggled past it and remained calm. "You haven't mentioned him, so I figured he pulled out," she managed.

"No, I had Arilyn help me put him through the matching system and we did a few cross-checks with our client base. He's not the type to enjoy a mixer or a stream of first dates. I needed to put it on the line with one big match. And I think I found her!"

Izzy turned away fast, pretending to fiddle with papers so Kate didn't catch her expression. The sickness had turned into a dull fury. The idea of another woman coming near Liam made her turn vicious. "Umm, that's great. But how do you know this is his match?"

"Besides a perfect profile fit via the computer, she's a child advocate of the court system to help abused children find solid homes, and her father is a police officer, so she knows what to expect. She has no issues with cops—and I know a lot of women do. She's got a master's degree and she lives close to Verily. She's attractive and has a fabulous sense of humor, and guess what else?"

With each word, Izzy's temper grew, until her head got a bit foggy. "What else?" she growled.

"She has a dog! A beagle mix, just like Devine! Do you believe it? Their first date will probably be epic."

Izzy snapped her pencil in half and it went flying up in the air. Kate jumped back a step. Izzy grimaced. "Oops, sorry. Yeah, it'll be epic."

"Would you like to call him and tell him the big news? I know we're training you to deal more personally with clients. You can even schedule their date if you'd like."

Izzy gnashed her teeth. One of the folders crumpled in her grip, and she had to take deep breaths to release her fingers. Schedule a date with Liam and another woman?

Fun.

She opened her mouth to tell Kate to stay far away from

her man, then froze. What was she doing? Isn't that what she wanted? To set him up with a woman who could give him everything he needed? She practically choked on her response. "Sure."

A pause. "Wonderful. Why don't you try that new Japanese restaurant on Main Street? I heard it's got great food and it's pretty romantic."

The room tilted. Raw emotion battered her in waves. *Never.* "Sure," she said again.

"Excellent. Doesn't it feel good to finally set Devine up with a woman who's going to care for him? I have a feeling they'll have great sexual chemistry, too. Stone said Devine likes blondes."

Izzy gripped the edge of the desk and prayed for sanity.

"Well, I'm off to an appointment. Let me know when you've finalized the date. I've left Brittany's number in the contacts folder so you can call. Bye!"

Kate left. The bells tinkled merrily on her way out.

Brittany? Really? She couldn't believe he preferred blondes. He'd never told her that or even indicated his preference for blondes. And she was a child court advocate? Ugh—it gave her a cavity. Someone dedicating her life to helping those poor children was just too much. She had to have some kind of horrific skeleton in her closet. Maybe she was really a jealous maniac and would stalk Liam. And how did Kate know she had a good sense of humor? Liam's humor was very particular and she might not get it.

No, she wouldn't do it. Couldn't do it.

As the hours passed, she tried to pick up the phone a hundred times to make the call. She'd just schedule the damn date and let them be happy in their perfectness. They'd had a great month. Did she really think it could last?

By the end of the day, she was bottled up and ready to explode. When Liam texted her about coming over, she ignored him. Screw him. Trying to date blondes behind her back? Whatever.

She walked Leia several times and started dinner. After ignoring two more texts, she was ready when the bell rang. She marched over, flinging the door open.

Liam held Han in one hand and set him down. With a yelp, he scrambled across the wooden floors, crashing into Leia, and they tumbled together in greeting. "Why didn't you answer my texts?" he asked in puzzlement. "I was going to pick up sushi for us if you didn't feel like cooking."

"Oh, sushi. Convenient."

He scratched his head and shut the door behind him. "Umm, yeah, it was supposed to be convenient. What happened? You look ready to pop, and not in a good way. Did Leia destroy something else?"

"Why didn't you tell me you liked blondes?"

He walked to the kitchen, grabbed a glass, and poured himself some lemonade. "Blondes? I don't like blondes."

"You lie! Kate said Stone said you preferred blondes over brunettes!"

"What the hell are you talking about? Have I dropped into some time warp or something?"

"Forget it. I don't care that you like blondes! I hope you and Brittany are very happy together in your perfect lives."

His blue eyes flashed with matching temper. He slammed the glass down and stalked over to her. "Who the hell is Brittany?" he yelled back. "Have you gone insane?"

She jabbed a finger at his chest. "Brittany is your match at Kinnections! Your perfect match, according to Kate. She wants me to set up a date with you at the Japanese restaurant. Congratulations—your profiles fit and supposedly she's hot, so you can have ridiculously good-looking Ken and Barbie babies!"

He grabbed her by the shoulders. "You've lost your mind. I never asked Kate to set me up on a date after I had to bribe you to go to dinner with me. I have no interest in dating anyone else but you!"

"Bullshit," she shot back, fisting his shirt in her hands. "She's everything you've been looking for. Blonde, a child advocate, a family in law enforcement, and she has a damn beagle. Kate said it's meant to be and I know you want to meet her, so go ahead. I don't care!"

He twisted his fingers in her hair and yanked her head back. Leaning over her with pure male fury, he spoke deliberately against her lips. "Listen up and listen good. I already found everything I'm looking for and it's not in some fucking computer with some perfect stranger. It's with you, even though you're certifiably insane."

Caught in the rising storm of adrenaline, she leaned forward and bit his lower lip. He cursed and she glared at him, her body on fire, her core softening and heating like lava. "Get out."

She knew it was an order he'd never obey. He also knew she didn't want him to, so he tightened his grip on her hair, thrilling her with the edge of anger and raw, sharp desire. "I'm going to do two things right now, Isabella, and there's not a damn thing you can do to stop me." In one move, he ripped open her shirt, popping buttons everywhere. Her chest heaved for air. Her breasts swelled under her tiny white lace bra. "I'm going to fuck you till you're not mad anymore. Then I'm going to hold you until you know I'm not going anywhere."

His mouth crashed down on hers.

The kiss was wild and fierce. They ripped at each other's clothes, falling on each other like starving predators, all tongues and lips and teeth, until he lifted her up high and slammed her back against the wall. Deftly unbuckling his belt, he yanked down his jeans and sheathed himself, never breaking from the deep, wild kiss. She moaned, clutching his shoulders as he pushed up her skirt and pulled off her panties. With one quick, graceful movement, he lifted her high, then brought her down in a stunning move that joined them deeply together.

"Liam!"

She kissed his neck, sunk her teeth into his shoulder, and hung on while he took her on a wild ride that left no shred of doubt she belonged with him. Shoving her hips upward for more, he worked his fingers to her clit and rubbed, and she came hard, screaming her pleasure as she convulsed around his cock.

He followed her, grunting her name, still pinning her tight against the wall so every curve cushioned his hardness. Slowly, he slid her back down till her feet touched the floor. Izzy clung to him, her knees weak and unable to hold her up.

And then he kept his second promise.

Scooping her up into his arms, he walked over to the sofa and settled her in his lap. Curling her into his embrace, pressing her face against his damp chest, he crooned her name and held her tight, stroking her hair, and she began to cry, because she knew she loved this man and she still didn't know what to do.

DEVINE HELD HER for a long time. Every tear she shed broke him slowly apart, but he refused to interrupt the sacred moment. Something had shifted between them—an opening up he hadn't felt before.

He loved her.

God, how he loved her. It was like finding his other half. There was no doubt, or fear, or tension, regarding the knowledge. Just a simple acceptance and gratitude. But it still wasn't the right time to tell her. He knew Izzy's self-doubts ran deep, entwined with who she was and what she believed he deserved. The only solution was to keep moving forward. Knowing she'd been crazed with jealousy only confirmed his belief she loved him just as much. The truth sang in his blood and seeped into his skin. His soul recognized her love for him. So he'd wait for the words and wouldn't complicate things by telling her of his own feelings.

Right now, she needed comfort. Holding her soothed him on a deeper level, allowing his soul to breathe. He reveled in her scent, kissed her tears away, and waited for her to calm down. Finally, she turned a tearstained face up to him, wet blue eyes gleaming with confusion and want.

He smiled. "Want to finish cooking dinner?"

She blinked. Then her swollen lips curved upward and sunshine drenched his vision. "Yes."

"Then let's do it."

He eased her off his lap, stood up, and offered his hand.

She took it.

For now, it was enough.

eleven

EY, BABE. LONG TIME no chat."

Izzy lay stretched out on her bed, feet dangling over the footboard, Leia resting on her stomach. The puppy's head was nestled in between her breasts, and her sweet breath came out in little snorts. Izzy had finally placed a call to Raven, guilty they hadn't updated each other in a few weeks.

Her best friend chuckled over the phone. "'Bout time you called. I miss you like crazy. When are you coming to Harrington to see my bar?"

Raven had bought a bar/restaurant called My Place. With her skill for cocktails and the Culinary Institute Academy graduate chef she'd snagged, the bar was becoming a huge success. Izzy was so happy to see her friend's dreams finally come true. It had been a long road for both of them, with lots of bumps and errors, but without Raven, Izzy doubted she'd be clean and sober and happy right now.

"Soon. Guess what I got?"

"A hot man?"

"A puppy! I named her Princess Leia. She's a beagle-basset mix and the cutest thing ever."

"Aww, text me pictures right now! I can't wait to meet my new honorary niece! Is she wrecking your house?"

"Yes, but I don't care. Are you doing okay over there?"

She sighed over the phone. A few seconds of silence ticked by, which told Izzy her friend wasn't ready to confess something yet. "Kind of. Things have been . . . odd. Let's just say the next time we chat I may have more news for you."

"A boy?"

"Girlfriend, when isn't it a boy? But this time it's even more. I'm just not ready to share yet. Are you cool with that?"

"I'm always cool with you. I'm here whenever you're ready—day or night."

"Sunset to sunrise," Raven echoed, words they always spoke in their friendship pact from years ago. "What about you? Boy trouble?"

"Yeah. A guy from my past showed up in Verily. I'd hooked up with him at a college party six years ago. Imagine my surprise when he walked into Kinnections."

"Did he remember you?"

"Yeah, he did," she said softly. "Seems we both had a hard time forgetting each other."

"Doesn't sound like a problem so far," Raven said slowly. "What's the deal? Is he married? Engaged? Girlfriend?"

"No."

"Cheater? Liar? User? Dickhead?"

"No."

"Then why do you sound wary?"

"'Cause I kind of love him," she choked out.

"Isn't that good? If he's not an asshole, why do you sound upset? Does he not feel the same way?"

"No, I think he does. But he knows I used drugs, Raven. And he's a cop. A rule follower. He's gorgeous and kind and good-hearted and perfect. We'd be terrible together."

"Umm, babe, you've been clean for two years. You have a great job. You're back with your family. What's the problem?"

Izzy chewed at her lip. It was hard to explain the demons that still lurked inside of her. As if one day they'd be tempted out of the darkness and she'd break and be back exactly where she was. This time she'd take everyone with her. Did Liam really deserve that type of love? With a woman who always seemed to search for disaster?

She wasn't ready to spill her secret fears yet. "I guess I'm just freaked out. I haven't been involved in anything serious my entire life."

"Yeah, it's scary as hell. Listen, just remember you're worth everything great in this life, Izzy. Don't forget it. He'd be lucky to score a chick like you."

Izzy laughed, relaxing a bit. "Thanks. I'll send you pics and call you next week. Peace out."

"Peace out."

The phone clicked.

Maybe Raven was right. Liam had told Kate he was pulling out of Kinnections because he'd met someone, but he refused to share who. Thankfully, Kate never questioned Izzy about it. Though they had never announced an official relationship, Izzy began to wonder if she should tell her friends. She'd finally confided in her sister and swore her to secrecy, but maybe it was time to make it more official. Maybe she could continue being with Liam with no complications.

Her phone vibrated. She smiled and hit the button. "Hey, where are you?"

She heard the roar of masculine voices in the background. "I'm over at Ray's Billiards. We had a major bust today and I'm celebrating with the guys."

She laughed. "Congratulations! I can't wait to hear about it. Take your time; if you want to party tonight, I can always come and pick you up. Or we can just see each other tomorrow."

"Hell, no," he growled over the phone, lighting up all her girly parts. "Why don't we go to dinner and celebrate? Can you pick me up at Ray's?"

"Sure. Give me twenty minutes."

"See you then."

Humming under her breath, she freshened up, slipping on a pair of designer jeans, high-heeled boots, and a scarlet sweater that left her shoulders bare. She spritzed herself in Light Blue by Dolce & Gabbana, donned a pair of gold hoops and her favorite gold skull necklace, and got Leia tucked away in her crate with her favorite bone.

Cranking up the music loud, she car-danced, thinking over Raven's words. The past weeks had been so good with Liam. Maybe she needed to let go a bit and be kinder to herself. Yes, she might be afraid of screwing things up, but she was in love with him. Wouldn't that be enough to fight the demons? How could she possibly walk away from everything good between them?

She pulled to the curb, parking down the street from Ray's. When she entered, the sound of Irish music, loud male voices, and clinking pool balls met her ears. The familiar scent of beer and whiskey rose to her nostrils. She always thought the place had a great homey feel, where you could grab a good Guinness, listen to some music, and play a few rounds of pool or darts with friends. She spotted Liam with his crew at the far back and held up her hand. He must have changed out of his uniform, because he wore a green Henley, jeans, and sneakers. A Key West baseball cap was turned backward on his head. He looked both sexy and adorable, and her heart leaped.

"Hey, Isabella. Come meet everyone."

When she reached him, he pulled her into his arms and kissed her solidly. The loud wolf whistling was secondary to the roaring in her ears. She hadn't expected him to declare their relationship so publicly. Stone crossed his arms in front of him and glared at them both.

"You didn't tell me shit," he accused. "How long has this been going on?"

Izzy shifted her feet, an odd blush heating her cheeks.

Holy crap—she never blushed! "Just a little while. The girls don't know yet either."

"Well, I'm telling Arilyn tonight, so you better spill the beans tomorrow."

Liam laughed. "You're such a gossip queen."

"Screw you, Devine. I just like information. It gives me power."

Izzy tried not to laugh at their banter. She'd learned Liam's language descended into grunts and curses around his male buddies. It was another part of him that fascinated her, along with his delicious dominance in the bedroom that often sprung up to surprise her.

Liam pointed out the three other men with him. "This is McCoy, Make It Work Dunn, and the Rookie."

Her lips twitched. "Hmm, interesting. Do you think I can have their real names?"

Liam shrugged. "Sure. This is Jason, Tim, and Patterson."

"Nice to meet you."

They all welcomed her with warmth. "Beer, wine, or cocktail?" Jason asked.

"Seltzer with cranberry juice would be great."

"Got it." He moved to the bar to grab her drink and Liam wrapped an arm around her waist, holding her close. Warmth and security suffused her. She felt like a . . . girlfriend. And it was nice.

"So, fill me in on this bust," she said. "Unless you can't talk about it."

Tim groaned. "Here we go. Are we gonna have to hear about this epic bust for the rest of the damn week? I'm bored already."

"Get over it," Stone said. "You're just pissed you and Rookie couldn't even get your speeding-ticket quota."

Liam laughed. "Stone and I were patrolling our normal route and we see this guy running down a side street and jumping a fence. We got curious, so we parked and went after him."

Stone cut in. "I never knew the woods went that fucking deep! I'm talking serial-killer sheds could be hidden in there. I swear, I plan on staking out the woods more often."

"We don't have money for stakeouts," Jason interjected, handing her the drink. "You think you're back in the Bronx, Petty?"

"You're not sulking about pulling crossing guard duty, are you, McCoy?"

Jason stuck up his middle finger.

Liam took up the story without missing a beat. "So we follow the guy out to this building and there it is, right in front of our faces. A meth lab. I'm talking *Breaking Bad* here—they had everything they needed to crank out some serious stuff."

"So we call it in, keep a watch on the place, finally make the bust, and end up arresting three main guys and confiscating a crapload of meth!" Stone crowed.

"It was a thing of beauty," Liam said.

Tim made gagging noises and Jason stuck up his middle finger again. Patterson gave a mournful sigh.

Izzy broke into laughter. She loved seeing Liam in his world. He held a comfortable, close dynamic with his work buddies. She squeezed him hard. "Congratulations. It certainly sounds like a thing of beauty to me."

"Oh boy, Hollywood, you really pulled the wool over her eyes," Jason said.

"At least I didn't have to blindfold her and beg her to marry me like you did, McCoy," Liam teased. "How many times did she turn you down before she got weak and agreed?"

"Twice, only twice! Now stop distracting me. I'm one game up and I want my damn twenty dollars. Finish up."

Liam winked at her, gave her another kiss, and shook out his hands. "Watch the master in action, sweetheart. I'm gonna win our dinner money tonight."

"You taking your lady out to the taco stand again, Hollywood?" Tim called out.

She chatted with Tim and Patterson, telling them they'd met via Kinnections and sharing easy conversation. "We like to rag on him but you're with a good guy," Tim said, taking a sip of his beer. "Known him for four years now."

"I gather there's not a lot of huge busts going on in Verily to get excited about," she teased.

"Nah, we do pretty good here keeping the crap off the streets. Meth is getting more popular, though. Bastard junkies will do anything to get their fix." Loathing flickered in his eyes. "I'm so sick of their weepy stories. They give you excuses about their horrible past and how they couldn't help it, but each one of them decided to snort or smoke or stick a needle in their arm because they're weak."

Patterson nodded. "Yeah, then they do their rehab stint, promise they're gonna be good, and they're back at it again."

"Junkies disgust me. They're ticking time bombs better left in jail so they can't hurt any other people when they explode."

Her stomach lurched. The two men across from her held similar expressions. She swallowed, fingering her straw. "You don't think some of them deserve forgiveness? If they don't do it again and try to build a respectable life?"

"Once an addict, always an addict," Tim commented. "I know I'm not politically correct and people would give me shit, but it's the truth. In all my years as a cop, I haven't found one person who was able to stay clean. Eventually, the demons come get them and it's all over."

The demons come get them.

The room swayed, then settled. An icy knot formed in her belly. The cold spread through her body, numbing her.

Once an addict, always an addict.

"Sorry, I get worked up over that topic. Anyway, nothing you need to worry about. You're good for Hollywood. Now I know why he's been so damn happy at the station lately."

Patterson agreed, and they chatted a bit, but their words

were a distant roaring around her. All she could hear were the same words repeated again and again in a horrific mantra that described her life.

A shout went up from the pool table, and Liam high-fived Stone. "Winner, winner, chicken dinner," he sang, pocketing his twenty.

"Yeah, enjoy eating at KFC, Isabella," Jason called out.

She forced a stiff smile, and they said their good-byes. She got in the car and knew she couldn't do it. She couldn't go to dinner and pretend it was all going to be okay. Because it wasn't.

Izzy cleared her throat. "Umm, Liam, do you mind if I just drop you off at home? I'm not feeling too good."

"I'm sorry, sweetheart. What's wrong?" He reached over to touch her but she shrank back. He paused, his stare hardening. "Isabella?"

She started the car, swallowing. "I just—I just need some time off tonight. Time for myself. You understand, right?"

His voice was pure ice. "Sure. I understand completely."

He didn't speak as she drove to his house. With damp, shaking hands, she pulled up to his driveway and waited. She needed desperately to retreat and think. When she was around Liam, he made her mind fuzzy, because the only thing that mattered was being close to him. The door opened, then slammed. She half closed her eyes, willing herself to keep it together, and moved to put the car back into drive.

He tapped on the window. Slowly, she hit the button and lowered it.

"Get out of the car, Isabella."

His command lashed sharp enough to draw blood. "I just think—"

"Now. I refuse to have this conversation in a car."

She got out and stood up straight. He was right. Dear God, he deserved for her to tell him the truth face-to-face. She couldn't slink away just because things got hard. The last month had been like a dream, but she'd known it couldn't last. Reality always intruded in life. "You're right; I'm sorry."

"Inside."

She followed him in. He took Han out of the crate, walked him quickly, then settled him with some food and toys while she waited in silence. He tore his cap off, tossing it to the side, fisted his hands, and turned to face her. "I want to know what happened in the bar."

She took a deep breath. Every word she spoke was like an ice pick in her heart. "I was talking to Tim about drug busts. He was expressing his opinion about addicts—junkies—who he believes are the scourge of the earth and don't deserve a second chance. He mentioned something that has been bothering me for a long time."

"What?"

"That the demons always come back. And he's right. I can be tempted at any time. Something can fall apart and I can use again. It's something they teach us right away. He said, 'Once an addict, always an addict.'"

Liam cursed viciously. "Listen, Tim has seen some bad things out there and has no experience with anyone close to him using. Are you telling me Tim's opinion—someone you just met—was important enough to want to run back home without even talking to me?"

Shame filled her. She lifted her chin. "No, you're right. See, I get like that when things get hard sometimes, Liam. I twist things up in my mind, and then I hurt people."

"Isabella, spare me your litany of sins in your quest to save me. I'm getting tired of it."

Anger curled inside, hot and satisfying and clean. "Oh, you're tired of it, huh? Maybe if you would begin listening to me, you'd see the problem with a future for us. Why do you think I tried so hard not to begin this thing between us? Because it would be too hard to stop!"

"Then let's not stop," he retorted. "Just because we decided not to talk about what we have doesn't mean it's not real. I played your game because I was afraid to freak you out. Well, now I'm done trying to hide my feelings for you. All we have to do is keep moving forward. Work through things that come up. But dammit, you need to talk to me when something upsets you. I can't be the only one fighting for us."

"There can't be an us!"

"Because you won't allow it!"

They faced each other. The past reared up and swallowed her whole. Images of her naked on the street. Memories of glorious lines of pure-white powder and parties that turned from night into day and night again. Recollections of her sister's face when she lashed out with her venom, and her parents' disappointment, and Raven's choking sobs when she thought she'd overdosed and begged her to seek help. Years of abusing and neglecting herself physically and emotionally. How could she possibly be enough for this man she loved more than her own life?

And she did love him. Oh, how she loved him, from the very depths of her broken soul.

"Tim reminded me of something I've always known," she said. "He said addicts are always ready to explode again. I can't give you any guarantees. I have to accept myself for who I am, flaws included."

"There are never any guarantees in life. In love. In anything. Does that mean you'll never allow yourself to love?" he challenged. "Are you going to protect the entire world from the disaster that is Isabella MacKenzie, or am I just your one lucky winner?"

"I don't know! I never thought about falling in love with someone like you! You're a police officer. What would your family say if they found out about my past? Your cop buddies?"

"Who cares? My family will see how happy I am with you and won't care. As for my friends, why do we need to tell them anything? It's our business. Hell, I'm proud of what you went through! I'm proud to stand by a woman who took life by the fucking tail and turned her devastation and darkness into healing and light. And every damn time you devalue yourself, you devalue me. Us. And I can't take it anymore, Isabella."

He closed the distance and yanked her into his arms. Cupping her face, he kissed her, forcing her lips to open to his, sliding his tongue deep into her mouth, and claiming her completely. She moaned, helpless to fight him, her body softening beneath him and flaming to life. When he finally ripped his mouth away, he was breathing hard, a fierce blue flame glinting in his eyes.

"I love you. All of you—past, present, and future. I tried to play it your way so I could prove to you how right we are for each other. You, my love, are the other half of my soul. But for this to work, you need to fight for me, too. You need to believe in yourself as much as I do to give us a chance. Do you love me?"

She clung to him, terror washing over her. "Yes. I love you. I think I've loved you from that very first night."

"Then it's time for you to make a choice. Don't walk away from a future because you're afraid of the past. Don't sacrifice our actual happiness for some mythical perfect happiness out there with someone else that doesn't even exist."

She looked into his beloved face and saw two roads

ahead of her. One filled with laughter and love and uncertainty. The other cold, empty, but safe. Secure. If he wasn't willing to save himself, she had to do it for him. Just like she'd always known from the beginning.

Izzy took a step back. "I love you too much, Liam. You need to be with someone who's completely whole. Someone you truly deserve."

Silence crashed between them. The grief and pain in his eyes felt like knives stabbing into her skin, drawing blood. And then he was turning his back as if he couldn't bear to look at her.

"I need you to go now," he said quietly. "But don't forget, this was your choice. You gave up on everything because you didn't believe in yourself. And I can't fix that for you. No one can."

The numbness came back to mask the pain. She turned and left, shutting the door quietly behind her.

twelve

"HI, DADDY."

"Hi, pumpkin." She held a little bit tighter to her father's embrace, and as if he sensed she needed extra comfort, he held her for longer than usual. Her smile was wobbly but still firmly in place. At this point, she needed to be around her family to fill the emptiness.

She walked into her family home where familiarity wrapped around her. From the spiral staircase to the elegant open foyer, she stepped back in time where her childhood reigned supreme. Pale-yellow walls, furniture now battered from the war of time, the family room beckoned with its cozy rug, overstuffed furniture made for comfort, and the solid coffee table that had held hundreds of platters. Amazing aromas drifted from the Tuscan kitchen where her mother ruled.

"Aunt Izzy!" Her niece Taylor came over to give her a hug. Her gorgeous blond hair spilled to her hips, and her wide blue eyes were now edged with mascara and eyeliner. Now a young teenager, her face had filled out, along with other parts. "How is it working at a real matchmaking agency? Have you met any cute guys?"

Izzy ignored the flare of pain and smiled at her niece. "Not yet, but I'm sure I will. If dating becomes too disastrous, you can grab the friends-and-family discount."

Her sister-in-law, Gina, walked in with her brother, Lance. "Please let's not discuss dating. I'm still working on negotiating curfew."

Taylor sighed with exaggerated patience. "M-O-M! I told you Sarah gets to stay out till eleven and you want me to be home at ten. I'm not a baby!."

"School nights ten. Weekends eleven," Lance cut in. "Discussion closed for now."

Taylor huffed but didn't respond. Gina gave her husband a warning look, but he winked at her, tugging playfully at her hair and getting her to smile. The crash of objects hitting the floor echoed in the air with loud voices. Maria skidded in, throwing herself into Izzy's arms with no doubt she'd be caught. Izzy covered her with kisses and heard her other niece, Lily, patiently explaining to her father that deer were animals, too, and not just ridiculous death hazards on the road.

"What happened?" she whispered to Maria.

Maria gave a very adult sigh. "Daddy almost hit a deer, and got mad, and started saying hunters needed to do their job better, and then Mommy and Lily got upset and said they're God's creatures and that they were going to force him to watch *Bambi*. But I think that's very cruel. *Bambi* made me cry."

Izzy pressed her lips together to keep from laughing. "Me, too. Thanks, sweets."

"Welcome."

She turned and Alexa stood before her. "Just a little family drama," she explained, tugging off her coat. Her beautiful black curls tumbled over her shoulders in a familiar disarray. She clasped Izzy in a firm embrace. "I'm so glad to see you. Is Gen able to make it or is she cramming in extra shifts again?"

"She promised to make it," Jim MacKenzie announced, his hands already filled with thick Italian bread covered in tomatoes and mozzarella.

"Jim! Are you eating the appetizers before everyone gets here?"

Her father shoved one portion in his mouth and chewed fast. "No," he mumbled.

Nick came in with Lily. It looked like their discussion had reached a fruitful end, and they were hand in hand. "Hey, Izzy, good to see you." Her brother-in-law had captured her heart when she'd first met him at sixteen years of age. With his tousled golden-streaked hair, elegant features, and lean grace, she'd crushed on him completely. His love story with Alexa was legendary in the family, especially since they were able to pay off her parents' mortgage and pull them back from bankruptcy or being forced to sell the house.

He was a modern-day knight, and her sister was his queen. There was no one else she could think of who deserved happiness more.

Her father began bringing in the plates of appetizers, uncorking wine, and pouring Izzy's favorite drink, cranberry and seltzer with a twist of lime. Chatter ensued, food was picked at, kids raced around the rooms squealing and giggling in lighthearted play, and Izzy closed her eyes, savoring the moment of just being with family.

"I'm here! I'm here!" Gen rushed in with Wolfe at her heels. "You better not have eaten all the tomato and mozz!"

Maria MacKenzie popped out of the kitchen, shaking her head at her husband. "Genevieve, you know I always save you some on the side. Your father can't help it. The mozz balls make him lose his mind."

They burst into laughter, and Izzy greeted her twin and Wolfe, the love of Gen's life. With his wicked serpent tat that scrolled up his arm and neck and wrapped around his ear, his stinging blue eyes, and his overall hotness factor, he'd caused her some turbulence when they'd first met and she crushed on him hard. Of course, with her drug use, that crush had eventually turned vicious, especially when she realized her twin was his preference. Still, Wolfe never made her feel anything but accepted and loved in his circle, his forgiveness evident in his gaze and smile when he saw her. She had offered him a formal apology during her repentance steps, and he'd just hugged her and said he understood better than she could ever know. "How's Kinnections treating you?" he asked.

"I really love it. I think I actually see a future there."

"I'm so glad for you, Izzy." He squeezed her hand and she smiled at him.

"Thanks."

"If you two don't start eating and stop gabbing, I can't be expected to save all the plates," her mother warned, giving them a big smile to soften her words.

They snacked and drank, catching up on everyone's news. When Maria called them to the table, it was filled with all of their favorites for the usual Sunday feast. Bowls of pasta with gravy and meatballs, garlic bread, homemade ravioli, huge bowls of fresh salad drizzled with homemade dressing made of olive oil, infused vinegar, herbs, and of course more garlic. Izzy took some grilled eggplant and a small bowl of pasta, her stomach still not back to normal after her breakup with Liam.

Actually, nothing was normal any longer.

She walked around with a hole she couldn't seem to fill. She smiled and did her job at work, but the world around her had dulled, losing its interesting angles and sharp edges she used to enjoy. She spent most nights home with Leia and made sure to go to extra meetings in case her plummet urged her to use.

But there was no desire for drugs. No desire for anything. She just existed, and in between every action she thought of Liam and what she had thrown away in the pursuit to save him.

"You're not eating, Isabella," her mother observed.

"I had a big breakfast," she said, plastering a fake smile on her face. Everyone nodded, but her twin stared at her with pure suspicion.

After the ravioli-eating contest, they declared her niece Maria the winner and began to clean up. Halfway through, Gen motioned her to follow. Climbing the stairs, they went into their childhood room, still filled with youthful posters of cute pop stars, and still painted the color of Pepto-Bismol. They climbed up on the queen-size bed—which had been the only upgrade for guests—and sat cross-legged. Gen propped her face in her palm. "Tell me everything. Is it Liam?"

Izzy had already confessed to Gen about their first meeting, getting the puppies together, and falling into a dating-type pattern. But every time her sister tried to get her to tell her the real reason she was freaked out, Izzy changed the subject. "We broke up last week."

Gen sucked in her breath, studying her face. "Why?"

Izzy lifted her hands, choking back tears. "I did it. I broke up with him. I was terrified that we'd end up hurting each other. No, that's a lie. I was terrified I'd hurt him. Yes, I've been clean two years, but he's a cop, and I know how these things work. I met some of his friends at Ray's Billiards and one of them told me he despised drug users and that they were the scourge of the earth. He said addicts can go back to using anytime. And he's right. I'm dangerous."

"Wait—have you had the desire to use lately?"

"No. I met with my sponsor and attended an extra meeting but I'm fine."

"Okay, are you saying Liam didn't trust you not to use?"

"No, he told me to forget about what Tim said and he confessed he loved me and said he wants a future together. He said I was strong and brave and he didn't care about my past."

Gen scrunched up her face. "I'm confused. He said all that and you still broke up with him?"

Ridiculous tears stung her eyes. "Yes. I left him because I can't trust myself. I think he deserves better than me, Gen. I love him too much to hurt him."

Gen let out a broken cry and held her tight. "Poor baby; I'm so sorry. Listen, I can tell you a whole bunch of things that make perfect sense but I'm not you. I didn't go through your struggles and I can't pretend to know the answers. But I do know exactly who you need to talk to, Izzy."

She sniffed. "Someone as fucked-up as me? Who?"

"Dad."

Izzy looked up. Her sister gazed at her with a touch of sadness. "I haven't told him anything about Liam. Not even Mom."

"Dad went through something similar, and I really think you should talk to him. Will you do that for me?"

The idea of telling her father such intimate struggles was hard. She loved him fiercely, but after he'd left, she'd distanced herself for a long while, taking most of her teen years to fully forgive and trust him completely again. She wasn't used to sharing her heart with her father, especially when her twin had been her true confidante.

But her gut told her to go to him. She nodded. "Yeah. I think I will."

Gen pressed a kiss to the top of her head. "Go now. I'll cover you with the cleanup. You know Lance is going to be knocking on the door, whining because we scurried away before all the plates were washed."

Izzy laughed. "I love you, Gen."

"Love you, too."

Izzy went downstairs with her sister and found her father pretending to fiddle with the dessert tray. She knew he was only wasting precious time until the table was clean and he could steal the first few rainbow cookies. "Dad?"

He half jumped and looked up guiltily. "Oh, hi, honey. Just trying to help get dessert ready."

"Do you think I can talk to you for a second?"

He frowned, straightening up. "Of course. It's a mild night. Wanna go on the deck?" She nodded, and they walked out the sliding doors into the brisk fall air. They sat down on matching deck chairs and faced each other. "I'm trying not to be your mom and freak out. Can you just tell me nothing's wrong with your health?"

"Oh, no, Dad; I'm fine."

He let out a relieved breath. "Thank God. Okay, hit me with it. I'm good for anything else."

She smiled, clasping her hands together. "It's about a guy."

"I know that, sweetheart. I'm your dad. It's always about a guy."

A small laugh escaped her. "It's a long story."

He nodded, his kind eyes gazing at her with a steadiness that soothed. "Then you start at the beginning."

She did. Izzy told him all about the night they first met, leaving out the details, and took him up to the night she'd left Liam. When she finished, he contemplated her in silence for a long while, seemingly gathering his thoughts.

Surprise hit when he rubbed his face and she saw a glint of tears shining in his blue eyes. Her heart stopped. "Dad, are you okay? I'm sorry if I upset you."

He shook his head. "You have nothing to apologize about. I'm going to tell you a story, Izzy. I never shared this with you because you're my daughter, and there're certain things you shouldn't know about your father. When I left all of you and took off, I was in a dark place. You see, my entire life I felt as if there were these demons inside me, hidden somewhere but always ready to spring out. I never felt . . . fulfilled. I loved your mother so damn much. I loved you kids. But when I drank, something loosened inside and I thought I felt free. Powerful. It made everything better, and easier, or so I thought. The drinking got so out of control, your mother threw me out, and I took off. I had some terrible moments. I woke up in alleys sometimes. I'd work driving a cab, save up some money, then go on a bender for days.

"One day, I was driving a cab and picked up this lady to take her to Montefiore Hospital. On the way, she chatted about her life story and then asked me for mine. For some weird reason, I told her I had a family but I'd left them. She said the lure of the bottle was sometimes overpowering but that it was never too late to get my life back. Everything hit me at once. As I drove, I realized I despised myself so much I could never go back. I had lost everything that was important.

"She repeated her words again to me: *It's never too late to get your life back*. When I reached the hospital, she handed me a hundred-dollar bill and said, 'Take the first step, Jim. Get your family back.' Then she left.

"I don't know how she knew my name. I never told her, and my badge was in the glove compartment—I had never put it up. I sat there in the hospital parking lot for a long time, then drove back to Dispatch, took another cab straight to rehab, and checked myself in."

Izzy held her breath, hand pressed to her mouth. "You never told me."

"I know. It was a long road back. First I had to forgive myself. Make amends. Take the time to heal my insides, where all the bad stuff lay in wait. You know the process, Izzy. Meetings. Talks with your sponsor. One day at a time. Eventually I got there, and I was allowed to be a husband and a father again. So, let me ask you this. Do you think I deserved to get you all back?"

She jerked back. "That's a ridiculous question! Of course. It was horrible what you did and how you hurt us, but you've been with us every day. You earned back our trust. I am so grateful to have you as my father."

"And your mother? Do you think I deserved for her to give me a second chance? To spend the rest of her life wondering if I'd ever make another mistake and leave again?"

"Dad, she loves you. She made her choice, and you've never let her down. You never will."

"Then why are you not allowing Liam to make his choice?"

Her head spun. She stared at her father, trying to process his words and realizing the truth of what he was saying. God, she'd never thought of it like that. Liam tried to tell her many times, but she was too stuck on not hurting him.

"That night you showed up at the house high and I kicked you out for good, I was destroyed. Not because of your sins, but because of mine. I felt responsible and guilty. I thought it was my genes that were damaged and I was terrified I'd made you into what I had been."

"No. Look at Gen and Alexa and Lance. They're fine. It was me. Something inside me was . . . different."

"I know. You're like me. I hated it. Maybe that's why I was always so much harder on you than Gen. I thought I could save you, but I couldn't."

"Dad, there was nothing you could have done. I made my own path, and there were plenty of times I could have made other choices. I had opportunities not to use. I chose my path, and it has nothing to do with you."

"Yes, I know. But a father only wants to protect his daughter at all costs."

"I'm afraid," she whispered. "Afraid I'm not good enough for him. Afraid I'll hurt him. Afraid I'll be weak one day and use again and destroy everything."

"I'm afraid, too. But trying to protect people by being afraid is wrong and against everything they're trying to teach us. We're addicts, Izzy. But we're people, too. We screw up and cause pain, but we also fight through the bad stuff. We love fiercely and try hard and do everything we can to be the best of what we are. God forgives you. We forgive you. You told me you forgive yourself, but if that were really true, you'd let Liam love you."

Yes. She hadn't allowed him to love her. She'd pushed him away, refused to talk about their relationship, and generally belittled his feelings. Still, he stuck by her, wanted her, loved her. Even to the last second when she walked away from him.

Dear God, what had she done?

"Personally, I think Liam is very lucky to have you.

You're an extraordinary person. We don't realize that almost every person we meet has a story. Something in life tries to break them. Sometimes life succeeds, but if we fight back and eventually find redemption, do you really think we should be punished for the rest of our lives?"

No. She closed her eyes and reached deep inside, to that inner core of darkness that lay quietly in wait.

She found silence there. Kindness. And the knowledge she deserved to love and be loved.

"I know what I have to do now, Daddy," she said, opening her eyes. "Thank you for helping me."

She rose from the chair and hugged her father, and they held each other for a while.

"I expect him to be introduced at Sunday dinner next week," he muttered.

Izzy laughed and hugged him tighter.

thirteen

*D*EVINE PULLED UP to his driveway and froze.

Her car was here.

Dizziness overcame him. He stared at the closed door and wondered why she was here. It had been two horrible, painful, grueling weeks since she'd walked away from him, and he was still barely surviving.

Even Stone was worried. He'd brought over a casserole Arilyn had made, as if someone had died and food would make things right.

Something had died—his heart.

And nothing would make it right again.

He couldn't do this again. He'd fought as hard as possible and still lost. Because the battle was within her, and until she figured it out, he was helpless. And if she was here just for sex, well, hell, he was throwing her out. He was better than just a guy with a dick, able to give her a good time. He fucking loved her and she'd fucking left him. Hell, she could be standing naked in there, and he'd just calmly tell her to please leave, because he wasn't going through this type of agony again.

Love truly sucked.

Temper fueling his body, he got out of the car and marched into the house. It was time to take back his damn key, too, so she couldn't do any of these magical appearances to tear him up. Men had rights, too. Where was it written that women were always the ones who got stepped on and abused in a romantic relationship? Or used for sex and lighthearted fun?

He was done. *Finito*. Over and out.

Devine swung open the door, slammed it behind him, walked a few steps in, and got ready to demand she get the hell out of his house.

And then he saw her.

She was in a skimpy gold lamé bikini, exactly like in the scene with Princess Leia in *Return of the Jedi*.

Posed in front of the fireplace, Leia and Han tangled and playing at her feet, she stood before him in perfect, mouth-watering, Eve-like sensuality. His gaze roved over the thrust of her breasts and the tiny triangles that barely covered her nipples. Her tat sat perfectly on the top of her right breast. The slope of her stomach, the hourglass of her hips. A minuscule piece of fabric covered her pussy, just enough to make a man ache to slip his hand underneath to find the hot, wet honey beyond. Smooth, golden skin displayed her glory in the flickering light of the fire behind her. She stood with her legs braced apart, like a warrior princess ready to do battle.

Her hair was curled and let loose to run wild around her shoulders. Her lips were painted a deep scarlet, moist and ready for his kiss. She remained still with perfect grace, waiting for him to get over his complete shock that immobilized his feet but not his dick.

Oh no, not his dick. That appendage had grown to full staff and was trying to strangle itself in his uniform. She was his fantasy come to life a few feet away, ready for him to take her.

"Liam—"

"I forgive you."

He closed the distance between them, even as he was attacked by the joyous greetings of the twin terrors. They leaped on his feet, slowing down every step, but his gaze was focused on only her.

A husky, sexy laugh escaped her lush lips. "No, Liam, I have to tell you some important things first."

"How about later?"

She threw her arms out and backed up, shaking her head so those silky waves lifted and brushed her naked shoulders. The straps barely held her straining breasts. He wondered if he made her leap back again if her breasts would escape their confinement.

"Liam, wait! Please let me talk first and then you can do anything you want to me."

"Anything?" he growled. "You have two minutes. And talk simply, because all the blood has left my brain and gone elsewhere."

"I love you. I love you with my heart and my soul and my body. You are everything I've ever wanted in my life, and I've been stupid—so stupid and afraid. All this time I've been trying to protect you I've really been trying to protect myself. By believing I'd never be good enough, I had a rational reason not to take a leap of faith with you."

"I agree." He took a step forward. "Go on."

"I don't want to live without you. And maybe I'll always be scared of what could be, or of using again, but I refuse to insult me or you by embracing weakness. Because I'm not weak, Liam. I'm strong. And maybe I screwed up before and didn't choose you, but dammit, I'll never make that mistake again. I'll choose you every time. If you'll have me. If I'm not too late. And I'll do whatever I need to prove I'm not going anywhere ever again. Okay?"

"Okay."

He reached her, snagged her around the waist, and pulled her in. His kiss was animalistic as raw hunger tore through his system at the first hot, sweet taste of her. As his tongue thrust deep between her lips, she gave it all back to him, shoving her fingers in his hair and pressing her body flat against his chest. His hands roved over her half-naked body, starved for the feel of her, as the puppies nipped at their heels and jumped frantically for attention.

"If I had known this thing worked so well, I would've invested in it a while ago," she gasped, arching up and offering her delicious mouth for surrender.

"Where'd you get it?"

"Costume store."

"I feel dizzy. Gonna pass out if I don't get you to the bedroom. Now." He lifted her up high, and she wrapped her legs around his hips as he stumbled to the bedroom, the puppies following and almost tripping him a few times. He gave up grace for speed and pressed her down on the bed, his fingers furiously working to pull off his uniform while he pressed kisses over her neck, her breasts, her stomach.

Gently, almost reverently, he pulled off the golden fabric and bared her to his eyes. "So fucking beautiful," he whispered, taking in her rosy-tipped nipples, the gleam of moisture between her legs. He touched her everywhere, swallowed her moans with his kiss, and pushed her thighs far apart as he poised by her dripping entrance.

"Tell me what I need to hear," he demanded, pushing in a few inches before he stopped, relishing the thrash of her head and the jerking lift of her hips. "Tell me."

"I'm yours, Liam. No more running. I love you."

"About damn time."

He pushed in and seated himself deep inside her. Gritting his teeth against the fierce shocks of pleasure, he began to slowly move.

Interlacing his fingers with hers, he took the journey far up, where sensations and pleasure ruled and the connection between them burned bright and hot. Took her to the edge, and kept her there, drinking in her beloved face, thrusting hard, scraping against her clit once, twice, and then —

They shattered. Her cries filled the air, and he pumped his hips, releasing and binding this woman to him forever.

They came down to the reality of desperate barks and whines as the puppies tried frantically to jump on the bed. He pressed his forehead to hers and stroked back her sweat-dampened curls.

"I love you, Isabella MacKenzie."

"I love you, Liam Devine."

"Shall we complete our family?"

She smiled and his heart filled. "Yes."

He scooped up Leia and Han and they rolled and licked, climbing over them in a crazed tangle of joy.

And on his bed, with the woman he loved and the puppies who had stolen his heart, Devine finally felt complete.

epilogue

"Now, THAT IS an epic love story," Kennedy announced, sipping her apple martini.

"Agreed," Kate and Arilyn chimed in.

Izzy grinned and glanced around the circle. "I think so, too," she sighed. "Not many men would stick around that long."

"Oh, I don't know. Nate put up with a lot of my shit before I had to do something grand and surrender. Of course, I never thought of a gold lamé bikini. You're smart, girl-friend."

Her sister laughed and grabbed a piece of pizza. "Izzy doesn't play. When she decides to snare her man, she goes all out."

"Are you ever going to put poor Nate out of his misery and marry him?" Kate asked curiously.

Kennedy grinned. "Yep. In fact, I'm planning to ask him to marry me. It's going to be major. I figure he's waited for me long enough, and I'm ready for the ring on my finger and a white dress."

Kate jumped up and down, and Arilyn blinked away her tears. Izzy and Gen clapped with glee. "I'm so happy for you," her friends said, giving her a quick hug.

"Thanks, guys. I'm still freaking out but in a good way. I'm so grown-up now. Kate, are my martinis so bad you don't want to even try them?"

A blush stained Kate's pale skin. "Well, umm."

Arilyn gasped. "Oh. My. God."

Kennedy stared. "Are you?"

Kate nodded. "I'm pregnant!" she burst out.

Another round of squealing, hugs, and threatening tears came over them. Finally, they all settled back in, chattering nonstop.

They were all seated at the bungalow, sitting cross-legged in a big circle. The puppies had finally been put to sleep in Izzy's room, passed out from too much excitement with all the company. Kate and Arilyn had brought over Robert and Pinky to play, but the puppies had exhausted even them. Now the dynamic duo snored in the corner, with Pinky curled up on Robert's back, her small head perched in between the pit bull's ears.

Two pizzas plus an array of cocktails lay in the center of the circle. Music played in the background and *Magic Mike XXL* was muted on the television. It was a perfect night with all the women Izzy loved.

"So, is it time to talk about the love spell?" Genevieve finally asked.

The women all shared a look. Izzy gasped and clapped a hand over her mouth. "I forgot about that!"

"You did it, right?" Gen asked suspiciously.

"Of course—a promise is a promise. But honestly, you don't all really believe in that stuff, do you? I mean, Earth Mother?"

Silence fell. Arilyn finally spoke up. "Umm, I kind of do. I mean, I think it's mixed with the power of harnessing our secret desires and putting it into the universe, but it worked. For every single one of us. Did it work for you, Izzy?"

Her eyes widened. Shock hit her. She remembered every single one of the traits on her secret list. As she mentally checked them off, she realized Liam was the exact match of every single one. No. Not possible. Was it?

Yet she'd met him right after the list was created. How odd.

"Okay, yes, he's everything on my list," she admitted. "I just don't know if I'm ready to promote Earth Mother and love spells."

"And that is why no one else gets the book," Kennedy announced. "It served our purpose. We all found love. Now we need to destroy it."

"I don't know," Kate said worriedly. "What if Earth Mother gets pissed and reverses the spells and our perfect men become monsters?"

Gen shuddered. "I agree with Kate. Why don't we just hide it somewhere? Or give it to a used-book store?"

"Izzy, do you still have it?"

"Yep." She got up, scooped it off of the bookcase, and returned to the circle. The purple fabric cover looked innocent enough, but they all knew what lay between the pages.

Kate shuddered. "I can't touch it—gives me a shock."

Izzy tilted her head. "Do you still feel a jolt when you touch two people meant to be together, Kate?"

Her friend's grin was full of mischief. "Yep. And I felt it with you, Izzy. You and Liam."

"What?"

"Yep. That day you did his intake, I touched both of you and that's why I fell on my ass."

Izzy gasped. "But you tried to set Liam up with that awful Brittany woman from Kinnections."

"It was just a setup to push you toward him. I knew you were fighting it. Figured you could use a bit of help."

Kennedy burst into laughter. "Nice move, dudette. I love your quiet manipulations. Now, I know we agreed to never talk about it, but it's just us in the circle. I know you felt the connection between me and Nate, and Liam and Izzy. What about Arilyn and Gen?"

"Confirmed. Now I'm happy to say hopefully I'm done getting electrocuted when we all party together. Maybe I can officially retire from being a subconscious witch."

Arilyn pointed to the book. "What's the agreement, then? The book helped all of us. It deserves to be taken care of, maybe for another generation."

"Maybe you're right," Kennedy said.

"I found it at the secondhand bookstore," Kate said. "What if we wrap it up and send it out to another bookstore?"

"But which one?"

Arilyn grabbed her laptop. "I'll type in a search and we'll pick one at random. That way, the universe can work in the way it wants, and we've safely delivered it back out there."

"Love it," Gen squealed.

Izzy laughed. She still wasn't sure if she believed in any of it, but she adored her friends and would back them in anything. Even a love spell.

"How about the Ripped Bodice? It's actually a store that just sells romance novels! What do you think?"

"Hmm, even if they didn't want it, they respect books and would find a good home for it. Let's do it," Kate said.

"Great. I'll take it and send it tomorrow."

Arilyn took the book and stuck it in her purse, then rejoined the circle. "I'm so happy, guys," she sighed, looking around. "You know, I think we've all found what we've been searching for, haven't we? I really love you all."

Kennedy groaned. "A, you always get mushy when you drink."

"No, she's right," Kate jumped in. "This is special what we have. I propose a toast."

Izzy raised her cranberry and seltzer and touched her glass to the group.

"To love."

"To friendship."

"To us."

They clinked glasses and drank to the future, and to each other.

And to happy ever afters.

acknowledgments

WOW. THIS IS GOING to be a bit longer than my usual spiel. Let's get to it!

A big cyber-hug to my editor for guiding me through this entire Searching For series and loving it as hard as I do. Your advice was always stellar, and writing this final installment was bittersweet.

Thanks to the Gallery/Pocket crew for supporting the series in a variety of ways and being willing to try new things to reach readers. Thanks to my agent, Kevan Lyon, for all her guidance.

Special thanks to Maybelline Smith from the Probst Posse for helping me name my cute puppy terrors, Han Solo and Leia—it was perfect!

The Searching For series is close to my heart. I've been living with these characters nonstop for four years, and they've become my family. Writing *Searching for Disaster* was an amazing experience I don't think will be repeated. The words flowed out of me until I couldn't sleep or eat or do anything but write. So write I did, and I finished this book in ten beautiful, glorious days. Then collapsed.

I explored many themes in this series, from stuttering and eating disorders to drug and alcohol addiction, animal rescue, and emotional abuse. Each subject I tackled with reverence, research, and experience. Writing real and broken characters has always fascinated me, and I will continue to explore these areas in my future novels.

Thank you to all the readers who embraced these special women from Kinnections and followed their journey toward happy ever after. I feel like I'm a better person for writing this series, and I hope you continue to recommend these books to your friends.

May love and friendship continue to bless all of your lives.

Keep reading for a sneak peek at Raven's story in

any time, any place

Book two in the Billionaire Builders series

Available now!

prologue

RAVEN BELLA HAWTHORNE watched the casket drop into the ground. The rain caused the hole to look slippery, almost like a mud hill. When she was younger, she probably would've looked at the slope as a great adventure, letting out a big war-type chant while she hurled herself down over the edge as if it were a giant Slip 'N Slide. She'd climb out with a big grin, mud crusted on every part of her body, and her father would shake his head and try to scold her. Meanwhile, his dark eyes would glint with laughter, and Raven would know she wasn't really in trouble.

But now, her father was in the hole. She'd never see that sparkling humor, or hear his deep belly laugh, or listen to one of his lectures in that gravelly voice that reminded her of a big papa bear.

Because her father was dead.

Aunt Penny squeezed her hand, but Raven hardly felt it. The cold chill of rainwater seeped into her skin and her soul, burrowing deep inside and making a permanent home to rest. The crew of men in black suits with bowed heads recited a prayer as the casket disappeared for good.

People threw roses in the hole. One weeping woman clutched her rosary. The priest concluded the prayer service, telling Raven and everyone else not to grieve, because Matthew Albert Hawthorne was in heaven with the angels and was finally, mercifully at peace.

Raven stared at the priest. At the mishmash of distant relatives she barely knew and friends who seemed more focused on the scandal surrounding her father's death than on her. No, other than Aunt Penny, she was truly alone. And she didn't feel grateful, or happy, or humbled her father was with God.

Instead, Raven was filled with rage.

Her beloved father, who had been her entire world, was a liar and a cheat. The man who dragged her to church on Sundays and lectured her on saving her body for love and being kind to others and always believing she'd accomplish great things in this world had abandoned his only daughter to run away with another woman. A stranger.

If it hadn't been for the red light, her father and that woman would be in Paris, building a new life away from their children. Instead, they were both dead, lying in the cold, damp ground while she dealt with the stinging slap of betrayal. For the first time, Raven knew what it was to hate.

She hated her father. She hated the woman who had stolen him away. She hated the three sons the woman had left behind, sons who spread evil words about Matthew luring their innocent mother away, painting him as a charming manipulator who cared nothing about the bonds of family.

Her father's once spotless reputation now lay in tatters around her. People gossiped and stared and whispered behind raised hands about the single father who'd ruined two families by seducing the matriarch of Pierce Brothers Construction. Somehow, some way, Diane Pierce had become a martyr. Which made Matthew Hawthorne the only villain of the story.

So Raven hated and burned for revenge while she stood in the rain, nodding at well-wishers. She listened to Aunt Penny thank the endless line of people for offerings of food, prayers, and help in their effort to feel validated during someone else's tragedy. Finally Raven walked to the limousine and slid onto the smooth leather seat. As they pulled away toward her new life, Raven had only one thought:

Payback was going to be a bitch.

one

DALTON LOOKED AT the table in front of him and frowned.

It was all wrong.

Frustration nipped at his nerves. Sweat dripped down his chest, and the familiar scents of varnish and sawdust rose to his nostrils. He rubbed his head, staring at the sharp curves and clawed feet of the dining room table he was restoring for the Ryans. The lines were right. His hands trailed lightly and lovingly over the top and down each leg, sensing the quality wasn't the problem. Dropping to his knees, he crawled underneath to check further, but there were no skips and the grains were full and smooth. The shape was perfect. Then what was niggling at his gut that something was completely off?

He rolled to his feet, backed up, and looked at the table in the light.

Too dark. The Brazilian walnut finish blended into blackish tones.

All wrong.

The voice whispered from within, and as usual, he didn't question where the answers came from. He just followed where they led. His clients had insisted on the darkest finish possible for their new antique find, and if he rebelled against those instructions he'd be taking some heat.

From both the Ryans and his brothers.

And as usual, he ignored the warning, choosing to follow his gut.

It needed a softer finish. Brazilian chestnut would work. The color was fuller, which would round out the angles to illuminate the gorgeous curves and elegant dignity of the antique. They'd chosen wrong, but if he did it the right way, they'd agree.

Maybe.

He pushed away the doubt, grabbing the towel to wipe his stained hands and guzzle some water. The low hum of the central air wrapped him within the perfect temperature. He didn't mind the cloying humidity outside, since he was used to some sticky Northeast summers. But his precious wood needed care, and it did best under steady conditions. Humidity was known to warp grains. Sometimes he needed to protect the raw materials from Mother Nature's occasional temper, and he had no problem embracing artificial environments.

His brothers would make fun of him for that thought, so he'd never shared it. Just like he'd be taking their shit when he called the Ryans to tack on an extra day to deliver the table. Too often they perceived him as flighty and irresponsible. The three of them might co-own Pierce Brothers Construction, but it was obvious Caleb and Tristan still didn't believe Dalton could handle his part in the business. The past year had been rough, and they'd all grown much closer, yet Dalton noticed Cal and Tristan still treated him like an annoying younger brother. Sure, they respected his talent with woodworking, but they still refused to acknowledge his contribution to the bottom line.

They drove him batshit crazy.

He shook his head and trudged over to the workbench. He began cleaning up his tools, kicking up another cloud of sawdust. Dalton thought over the past year and how far they'd all come. When he'd first learned of his father's death and the will that forced him to move back to Harrington, Connecticut, to run the family business with his two older brothers, he'd been pissed off and betrayed. He'd been happy in California, starting up his own business and free from his father's brutal ways. Christian Pierce had ruled his family like an old Roman king—his way or no way at all. He'd refused to allow any changes in the business, and the only softness in the boys' lives had been their beloved mother, who'd kept the family together.

Until the fatal car crash that not only took her life, but broke Dalton's heart and shattered his hope that anything would ever be okay again.

Everything he'd believed in crumbled and left him in

ruins. Diane Pierce had been the force that made them whole. Learning she'd run away with a strange man, leaving her family behind, crippled them all. The two one-way tickets to Paris confirmed the betrayal. The only way to get through it was to imagine she'd been conned by the man who'd burned in the car beside her. Of course, he'd never get the answers he sought. They had all died with her, as had everything good and gentle and pure in his life.

After that, a perfect storm of horrific events tore them all at the seams until there was nothing left but anger and pain between them. Dalton fled to California, Tristan settled in New York, and Caleb remained behind to work with their father.

He tightened his grip on his saw. Five years and they'd barely spoken. Once so close to them, Dalton had lived in a void, as if he didn't have a family, until he got the news that Christian Pierce had died of a heart attack. When he'd returned for his father's funeral, the will had made fools of them all. Christian's will decreed all three of them needed to run Pierce Brothers at a profit for one year, or the business would be sold off. When Cal begged Dalton and Tristan to help, they reluctantly agreed, but it was a rough year, full of painful revelations and lingering resentment. They'd somehow managed to slowly rebuild until they'd become a family again.

When the year was up, Dalton made his choice to stay. His vision of running Pierce Brothers as a full partner filled him with pride and ambition. Now he was able to stand proudly next to Caleb and Tristan and call it a real family business. Caleb oversaw the new builds as the main contractor. Tristan dealt with real estate, design, and flipping houses. And Dalton was lucky enough to do what his life calling had always been: work with wood. Building pieces from scratch into treasured and beautiful objects soothed something within his soul. His hands were an extension of creativity and nurturing, and each piece was unique and special, as if he'd just stepped away from the wood to allow it to reveal the heart. The brothers had finally found their rhythm, and Pierce Brothers Construction had leapt to stellar status once again.

He just wished his brothers would stop shutting him out of the big decisions.

Dalton stored his tools carefully and straightened up his workshop. The large shedlike structure looked plain on the outside, but inside, it was his own personal paradise. Set back by the woods on the family mansion's property, it was completely private, surrounded by thick brush like a hidden fairy-tale house no one could find. Shelves covered the walls and were filled with various tools and scrap pieces. Each piece told a particular story Dalton treasured. His saw collection was legendary, and if anyone got too close, he actually felt a growl rumble from his chest. He might not be possessive of women, but grubby fingers better stay the hell away from his power tools.

Band saws, circular saws, and panel saws were his livelihood. Over the years, he'd added to his collection of lathes, planers, sanders, jointers, and routers. His machines were top of the line and lovingly cared for. An extension of his fingers, the right tool could make or break a job. A large multifunction worktable sat at the center of the room, with numerous drawers neatly labeled and tagged. He knew exactly how many drill bits lay within each compartment, and their sizes.

Cal had once "borrowed" a bit and forgotten to return it. After Dalton "mistakenly" shipped all the wood for a project to the wrong place in retaliation, his precious shed had never been touched again.

His favorite music was always at hand with his Amazon Echo; its digital voice assistant, Alexa, had lately become his favorite girlfriend of all time.

Dalton finished clearing his work space and glanced at his phone. He thought of his plans for the evening, which included picking up the new varnish for the Ryans and little else. Caleb and Morgan were going out. Tristan was away for a few days on a business trip. Maybe he'd call that pretty little blonde, Avery, and take her to dinner? His lackluster response told him it wouldn't be a good move. On their last date, he'd noticed she'd gotten that moony look in her blue eyes and had casually mentioned her sister coming to visit. Like she wanted him to meet her.

He fought back a shudder. Meeting any type of family

was a danger. Connections were made, and women got false ideas of where a couple of nights out could lead. Dalton hated hurting anyone, so he made sure the rules were laid out plainly for the women he dated so they knew where he stood. Unfortunately, too much time together equaled greater expectations.

That's when it was time to move on.

His gut burned with a strange hollowness that had never been there before. What he needed was a project all for himself. Too often he was doing cabinetry and decks for the specific houses being built, but they weren't his choices. Back in California, he'd been able to pick and choose the jobs he was passionate about. He was starting to feel like a factory worker rather than a woodworking artist. Sure, he knew it was part of being in the family business, and he prided himself on delivering pristine work. Though his brothers bitched about him not meeting his clients' demands, they grudgingly admitted that 99 percent of the time, the clients agreed Dalton was right and loved the outcome.

Yes, that was it. He'd keep his attention cocked for a special project that really meant something to him. That would take care of the itch and soothe the restless beast within.

He grabbed his shirt, took one last look around, and shut the door behind him.

about the author

JENNIFER PROBST'S novels, novellas, and ebooks range from sexy contemporary romance to erotica. She lives in upstate New York. For more about this multitalented *New York Times* and *USA Today* bestselling author, visit www.jenniferprobst.com.

Printed in the United States
By Bookmasters